RAY OF THE STAR

RAY OF THE STAR

BY LAIRD HUNT

COFFEE HOUSE PRESS

MINNEAPOLIS :: 2009

Coffee House Press books are available to the trade through our primary distributor, Consortium Book Sales & Distribution, www.cbsd.com or (800) 283-3572. For personal orders, catalogs, or other information, write to: info@coffeehousepress.org.

Coffee House Press is a nonprofit literary publishing house. Support from private foundations, corporate giving programs, government programs, and generous individuals helps make the publication of our books possible. We gratefully acknowledge their support in detail in the back of this book.

To you and our many readers around the world,
we send our thanks for your continuing support.

LIBRARY OF CONGRESS CIP INFORMATION
Hunt, Laird.
Ray of the star : a novel / by Laird Hunt.
p. cm.
ISBN 978-1-56689-232-2 (alk. paper)
1. Psychological fiction. I. Title.
PS3608.U58R39 2009
813'.6—dc22
1 3 5 7 9 8 6 4 2
FIRST EDITION | FIRST PRINTING
PRINTED IN CANADA

SECTION BREAK QUOTATIONS
I: *A Man Asleep*, George Perec
II: "Poor in the World," Bin Ramke
III: "Forgotten Underground," Christina Mengert

The author would like to acknowledge the support for this novel provided by PROF grant from the University of Denver.

Portions of this novel have appeared in
Mandorla and *Western Humanities Review*.

RAY OF THE STAR

I

Now you must learn how to last.

Then one day the deadly ones did appear.

THEY STOOD IN A SMOKING ROW AND TOLD HARRY WHAT they were going to do and Harry rose, trembling, and said that he would go, that they could take him, could please take him instead, but they just smiled, wisps of smoke escaping their already blood-soaked lips, then vanished, and Harry screamed and ran for the door, even though he was 500 miles from home and snow lay deep over the countryside and the world was a dead thing under the stars, so that later, as he stood in dark wool nodding at people who placed their hands on his arm and looked at him out of puffed eyes, he wondered why they weren't looking at him through ice, why ice didn't fall from their eyes and cover the floor and coat the walls, and end all warmth, and that later still it seemed to him that all warmth *had* ended and that the world around him had shrunk to the size of his fist and that the fist would never open again, upon which his wounded mind saw a fist bloom into a beautiful hand, and, with a crushed sob, he began to creep out of the sorry thing his life had become, but this was only after years had passed.

*L*EAVE, HARRY THOUGHT SO HE LOCKED THE FRONT DOOR, threw the keys into the snarled forsythia, got into his car and drove past houses he had long ago stopped looking at and did not look at now, and knew he would never look at again, and then they were behind him and the country beside the highway opened up, when there weren't any sub-divisions or industrial parks, onto cow-peppered grassland above which hawks circled and balloons hung heavily and gliders scraped away at the sky, an endless, hopeless affair the color of a postcard he had been sent, unsigned, some years earlier from a great city where he had once spent a few happy months, some kind of blue with a few drops of bloody red in it, which called to mind a drink he had once had but couldn't remember the composition of as he had sat in a bar in that great city and smashed himself to smithereens for no compelling reason, the way he had done many things in that particular part of his deep past, when he had worked hardly at all and slept a great deal and very little had mattered, much like, he thought as he took the exit for the airport, now, this moment, these last years, although the situations were not the same, oh no, even if very little now mattered and very little had mattered then there had been those intervening years when everything had mattered and that changed it, irrevocably, and as he walked away from his car, he thought again of the great city and that shade of blue, which had surely shifted over the

3 :: RAY OF THE STAR

years he had kept the postcard—part of a collection which even now, as he set his credit card down on the counter and said the name of the great city, was sitting, continuing to shift, in an Adidas box beside his desk in the house that years ago had stopped being his home.

On THE PLANE THAT CARRIED HIM OVER THE ATLANTIC HE sat next to a young woman with short hair the precise color, she informed him, of crushed pomegranate flesh, who was reading a coffee-table sized book called, *Exquisite Corpse: Surrealism and the Black Dahlia Murder,* which presented the argument, through neutral text and heavily inflected images, that the murderer in the famous unsolved case of Elizabeth Short was an amateur artist and physician named George Hodel, who was known to be a friend to and admirer of various surrealist artists, and it was certainly true, as the young woman explained to him over airline chicken, pasta, and peas, that the authors of the study made a credible case for their hypothesis, in part through the skillful juxtaposition of macabre crime scene photographs of the "black dahlia"—cut in half lying in high grass; cut in half lying on the autopsy table—with multiple famous surrealist canvases by Dali, De Chirico, Man Ray, etc. that showed women in various states of vivisection, all of which Harry found compelling and strangely moving, but not nearly as compelling and strangely moving as he found the young woman explaining all of this to him—this young woman with her deucedly bright hair and rather fat face and crooked teeth and pleasant voice and long earrings from the end of which dangled miniature blue skulls—and he said to himself, I hope she doesn't stop talking, but of course in time the stewards and stewardesses came and took away their massacred trays, and the young woman stowed her book and brought out a pair of headphones, and Harry, left alone with himself, began to fear that he would have one of his episodes and would have to go and lock himself in the bathroom, but instead he grew sleepy and stared at his hands and, legs twitching, eventually dozed, his head lolling ever-so-slightly from side to side, and every now and then he would wake and wipe his mouth and look over at the young woman and hope she would bring out the book again and talk to him, but she didn't, and, unable to come up with anything that felt even vaguely like a conversation starter, he was left to fill the long hours with empty thoughts, until, as he stood in line to use the restroom toward the end of the flight, a leather-faced man wearing a lapel pin with a fish motif about Harry's age embroiled him in a conversation about golf and an exciting new golf ball that was being released that very month, onto the central stem of which conversation Harry, for his part, pasted one or two remarks about Restless Leg Syndrome, from which he had suffered, increasingly, for years, as well as a new method for rendering certain objects invisible that was being elaborated in some cutting-edge laboratory somewhere, which conversation seemed to Harry to form an interesting echo of his earlier interaction about surrealism and the Black Dahlia, not least because almost from the moment the man had begun speaking to him about the issue of *Golf Digest* he was holding in his hands, he, Harry, had half-imagined that he was speaking to the Dahlia's presumptive murderer, George Hodel, which was why—hoping to draw him out and remembering something the young woman had said earlier about Hodel feeling "in his twitchiness," either untouchable or unseeable or both—he had interjected the comments about Restless Leg Syndrome and invisibility, but the man had more or less ignored Harry and had gone on about golf and then had stepped into a free restroom and had vanished by the time Harry came back out of his own cramped cubicle.

UPON RETURNING TO HIS SEAT, HARRY, WHOSE INTENTION had been to begin gathering his things—the unpromising copy of the *New Yorker* he had brought to read but hadn't opened, the half a Snickers bar he had stuffed between its pages an hour into the flight, the packet of salt and pepper crackers he had saved from his meal—instead leaned his head back, pushed the aluminum seat recline button, shut his eyes and found himself thinking, with startling immediacy, of footage he had seen on television the week before of a brilliant green tree frog with prodigiously spatulate toes and huge, heavy-lidded eyes negotiating the undulating upper canopy of an unnamed rainforest that stretched, like the surface of some improbable off-world ocean, in all directions as far as the camera could reveal, which gave way to a succession of treetop close-ups, first of what had looked to Harry like a cross between a caterpillar and a piece of delicate, white coral, then an enormous lizard that put him in mind, even though he knew he was dealing in gross approximations, of a Komodo dragon, then of an unmoving insect, also frighteningly large, with frozen onyx eyes and legs locked into aggressive right angles, then another tree frog, this one deep brown, that lowered itself, as the camera covered it, into a cave of wet bark, and as Harry sat there, as the plane adjusted its attitude and, quite palpably, began its descent, which prompted the attendants to begin moving about the cabin to collect garbage, and scattered passengers to lift their arms up into the half-lit, under-oxygenated air to adjust the overhead lights, it seemed to him that the trespass committed by the camera—held aloft by a specially designed airship, which would now make this previously under-explored territory readily available to science, not to mention, as the expression went, "the thousands of eyes hidden in every camera,"—had all the dimensions of a ghastly crime, one that wouldn't cease to expand in scope until it had ensured the destruction of this ocean of damp leaves and soft bark negotiated by the brilliant green tree frog, which, Harry suddenly imagined, turned its head, looked Harry in the eye, and smiled a bloody, Dahliaesque smile, he was sure had been as aware as its brown colleague that something unprecedented, if only dimly perceived, was nearby, and that this something must, at all costs, be hidden from, and while Harry might have continued to nourish this lugubrious line of thought, which he found strangely comforting, mired as he was and had been for so long in hopelessness, for the remainder of the flight, it wasn't very long before an attendant came and tapped him on the shoulder and asked him and the woman with the crushed pomegranate hair to put their seats in an upright position and to otherwise prepare themselves for the plane's impending return to earth.

AFTER NEARLY TEN HOURS IN THE RATTLING FUSELAGE, HARRY stepped off the plane into the smell of ocean, a salty thickness that became unpleasant, vaguely criminal, he thought, in its sweet, festering undertones, when, looking for the men's room, he walked down a flight of stairs that adjoined the baggage claim area into a bulging envelope of air that seemed very little better for breathing than the water in an overcrowded or forgotten fish tank, and he might well have fled immediately had he not, on regaining baggage claim, where the luggage was at last coming around on the conveyor belt, found himself again stationed next to the man he had spoken with on the plane, only this time the man was talking about the new ball to someone next to him whom Harry, too nauseous to turn his head and look, imagined was the young woman with the pomegranate hair, and that as the man described the new ball, which was to come in three colors and three corresponding qualities, the young woman was nodding but not really listening—who really listens in such circumstances?—as she watched for her bag, but of course Harry was wrong, it wasn't the young woman at all, as he discovered when, during a break in the delivery, a deep, accented voice said, "You could really lay siege to a course with a ball like that," to which the first man responded, "It'll be like assault and battery, I'm telling you, with this ball, life will be a siege," which series of extraordinary assertions got parsed and twisted in Harry's mind as he hefted his duffel bag and valise off the belt and onto a cart he had secured, then made his way past customs to the exit, into the phrase, "assault on life," which he rather liked, it seeming to represent the inverse of what he had been conducting for quite some few years now, and when he stepped outside into the sunlight, there was a fresh wind that swept out his mouth and nostrils and pleasantly filled the taxi he climbed into then out of in front of the building where, 1,000 years ago it now seemed to him, he had groggily, via the internet, rented a small apartment on a long, curving street, whose stone edifices, none built more recently than the late Inquisition, seemed to Harry, who was very close to falling asleep as he stood absently handing money to the driver, to be about to burst out of their own windows and come crashing down on his head.

DEEP SLUMBER SHOULD IMMEDIATELY HAVE ENSUED, BUT THE most annoying part of Harry's nocturnal disorder was that the greater his fatigue the more pronounced it grew, so that instead of immediately and gratifyingly giving himself over to oblivion after the long journey, he was obliged to spend the better part of an hour simultaneously resisting the urge to rip the affected flesh off his burning legs, which felt like an army of invisible termites was settling in for a long stay, or like someone had taken the content of an endless Tarkovsky movie and somehow shoved it under his skin, or like all the hair on his thighs and calves was growing inward at sickening speed, and doing vigorous knee bends and imprecise sun salutations and running through low-level logic puzzles—tedious things to do with knights and knaves—in an effort to trick his mind into thinking he was interested in being awake rather than asleep, which usually, eventually, gave him some relief, and as he went through this prolonged version of what, with certain variations, had over the years become his nightly routine, the low sloping ceiling he had already managed to smack his head against, the faded prints of deltas, root systems, and family trees that hung in worn-out frames from the walls, the dishes stacked precariously on shelves that were manifestly too small for them, the uneven tile that covered the floor of the kitchenette, seemed, as his mind mashed them together, like an extension of the interiors of the unpleasant air terminal and the rattling airplane and the house whose keys now hung in or lay under the forsythia bush, and it was hard not to think, with despair, about the remark a clerk at the local supermarket had made—when Harry, unprompted, had blurted out that he was planning to leave and probably forever—that it was "too bad we have to go with ourselves when we undertake such journeys," although he was quite surprised that when a few minutes later he sank onto his new bed, and began to drift, his thoughts turned not in the direction of the clerk's observation but toward a pair of wire service articles he had read just before leaving for the airport, the first of which had concerned a woman who had been stopped at a border somewhere in Gaza because of her unusual shape and was found to have wrapped three baby crocodiles around her stomach in an attempt to smuggle them into Israel, a discovery that had caused an apparently quite general pandemonium, comprised of screaming and running about, which image had actually been matched, if not exceeded, in its agreeable improbability, by the other article, which announced the recent marriage of the world's tallest person, and showed a picture of him standing with his new bride, who had her arm wrapped around his hips, and which as a kind of afternote, related the key role played by this really very tall person in using his long arms to remove chunks of plastic that had become lodged in a dolphin's stomach, and that would have killed it without his timely intervention, and as Harry made his way, panting slightly, into sleep, a wary but resolute Chinese giant with a trio of dolphins and a small Chinese woman strapped around his midsection led him there.

"Now," said harry, speaking to the mud-colored pigeon scrabbling away at the inhospitable roof's edge below him, and to the bits and pieces of clouds that were forever threatening, at least since he had been there—how many days had it been? not so many really—to coalesce into something dim and wet, "Now," he said again, "I will begin my assault on life," but *where* to begin: with a bit of hard sausage and some rosemary goat cheese and certainly a pickle and a bit of bread then some sparkling water, followed by a slice of apple and some additional cheese—blue this time—all of which and more Harry had procured that morning at the city's central market: a gigantic, cheery affair attended by red-faced, thick-fingered men and women who had seemed to him almost grotesquely happy to be hovering over their wares, which were no doubt fine enough, but still, surely not terribly profitable, not to mention constantly threatening to rot or tumble to the ground, plus there had been a chill in the air, something vaguely sinister, and already, even this early in the season, the smell of tour-bus diesel exhaust and brightly clad tourists following locals carrying clipboards and flags, a combination that Harry had found just irresistible enough to attach himself to a group of travelers from India, who after a time had looked at him with such collective fury that he had been obliged, or so it had seemed, to run away at top speed, his heavy bags bonking his knees, "Which means nothing," Harry said to the one-legged pigeon, "What do you know of happiness, or remember of it, not, I imagine, very much," and he brought one of the tiny pickles to his mouth then pulled it away again and turned from the window and the table and made for the near dark of the bedroom, where after staring at the crumpled heap of himself in a wall mirror for several minutes, he said, though without great conviction, "you must be mad."

Possibly mad, he wandered the tree-lined streets of the city for weeks, shivering along with the slowly growing emerald leaves, and the animals in the modern but poorly maintained zoo he visited three afternoons in a row, where the wild boars bloodied their tusks on each other and small children climbed into the penguin exhibit and frightened themselves half to death and the owls flung themselves over and over again into the rusted bars of their cages, and with the old women everywhere on the streets, shivering in their hats and sunglasses, one of whom, he thought, said, "Poor man," as she passed him, which, whether she had actually said it or not, made him laugh so hard he had to stop and lean against a lamppost, poor man, indeed: it was the acuity of this observation—whether or not it had been made by anyone or anything besides his bruised grapefruit of a head, let alone an old woman in a blue felt hat and long yellow coat dragging a handsome, though manifestly overfed Pekingese—its stunning incisiveness, which cut straight to the quick of his worn, unflattering outerwear, slumped shoulders, and rather saggy skin and vague, even sinister/vengeful puffery about assaulting life and so forth, with the result that as he continued his daily wanderings he realized 1) that given the level of sustained autoanalysis he was engaged in and no matter how much he might in his self-pitying, aspire to it, "mad" was probably inaccurate and that 2) well, there was no 2) but there might be, and that was something, maybe his sinister assault was underway after all, and how spectacularly interesting, and perhaps, well, perhaps it was time he took a little better care of himself.

GIVEN THAT OVER THE NEXT FEW DAYS HARRY CONTINUED TO agree with himself that better self-care was probably indicated, and convinced that both body and mind probably should, if something meaningful were to occur, be equally implicated by any eventual attentions, it struck him that he might well pay a visit to the acupuncturist whose more elaborate than average literature, which spoke of addressing just those things, had found its way into his mailbox, so he called and, almost before he had had a chance to finish his first explanatory sentence, was told to come over immediately, an injunctive that Harry was only too happy to comply with, and on the way over, sitting near the front of the bus, holding the acupuncturist's literature in his hand, which featured a series of awkwardly rendered but nevertheless appealing body-mind slogans, e.g., in approximate translation, "Have a Happy Way!" not to mention, in each of the accompanying photographs of the doctor and his office, the presence of the sort of bell to be universally found on hotel front desks—at least filmic representations thereof—and which Harry had always found most compelling, he felt quite sure that he had taken a promising step indeed, one that couldn't fail to help him, by dint of the renewed mental and physical vigor he would enjoy, to prosecute his assault,

"Come in," he was told by the very Doctor Yang pictured holding one of the bells in the literature he had carefully folded and accidentally left sitting on the bus,

"Many thanks for seeing me at such short notice," Harry said,

"Fill this out," said Doctor Yang, handing over a clipboard and asking him to ring the bell that sat on a little teak table next to a chair in the corner, for which request, despite its absurdity in the face of the petit office and Doctor Yang's continuing presence in the room, Harry was grateful, because it sufficiently mitigated the impulse the clipboard inspired—which was to immediately make for the door—for him to be able to make his way through the five or six pages of questions about his mental and physical health, which seemed so very poor on paper that, he thought, he might just as well go and lay himself down in the nearest meat locker, rather than on Doctor Yang's table, which is where, nevertheless, after dinging the bell, he found himself gazing up at a mauve-colored drop ceiling as Doctor Yang—who had looked at his chart, checked his pulse, and rather cryptically asked him if he ate a lot of pizza, "maybe too much pizza?"—inserted authentic thick needles into twenty-six points in his upper and lower body, which at least every other time made Harry jump, though Doctor Yang told him that this was a sure sign that the width of the needles and their placement was correct, that amateur acupuncturists who had not undergone sufficient training, or who were naturally sloppy—like the employees in a nearby practice he had recently infiltrated by posing as a patient and subjecting himself to their woeful ministrations—tended to use thin needles and incorrectly insert them, which was completely pointless, unlike what he was doing, which was serious and ancient medicine, whereupon, having offered these contextualizing remarks, he set one of the bells next to Harry's left hand and, giving it a cheery little whack, instructed him to ring it if he needed anything, and although Harry didn't do any more than tap the side of the bell with his left ring finger during the long hour he lay twitching on the table in the half dark listening to what he thought was Gaelic chant-ing coming through a boombox somewhere on the floor, the bell continued to accord him a sense not just of com-fort, but also of well-being, so that even though he was sure upon leaving that—although he had been happy enough to have had the experience—he would not make a return visit to Doctor Yang's offices for the long-term course of follow-up needlework that was recommended to him—what the fuck, in short, had he been thinking?—he did that afternoon procure a bell at an office supply store near his apartment, which he placed on his bedside table and would ring or imagine ringing from time to time in the coming days and weeks, and he did go out to a charm-ing restaurant near his house and order a large pizza, draped with asparagus and anchovies and drenched in extra cheese, which he ate with great appetite, while gaz-ing out the window at the handsomely clad passersby and wondering if, rather than looking into alternative forms of treatment, he shouldn't just go shopping.

YES HE SHOULD, HE THOUGHT THE NEXT MORNING, AND, giving his new bell a whack, decided to start by looking for something to replace the ill-fitting gray windbreaker he had dug out of the closet just before leaving, which, now that he was here in this city of smart sport coats, made him feel even older than he was, and which in collaboration with a bowling shirt, plaid trousers, and a park bench would have been all too perfect for pigeon feeding or coffin shopping, or so he put it to himself as he went up and down the mirror-lined escalators of a downtown department store, seeing himself over and over again from similar angles, none of them consoling, but before he could find men's wear, he was called over to a glittering counter by an extraordinarily fragrant salesperson holding up a bottle of crimson skin toner and a cotton pad, who, after remarking on the "energetic" patches of eczema around Harry's nose and mouth that were obscuring his finer attributes, worked his face over so vigorously with so many products that as Harry walked away with a bag of skincare items under his arm, he had the feeling that the salesperson had surreptitiously ripped off his face and replaced it with a lacquer mask, an impression that was not altered in the least by the sight of himself, again, in all the mirrors he was obliged to pass as he exited, suddenly too fatigued, despite the pleasure he had taken in being so assiduously scoured, after sitting there under the bright makeup lights and the salesperson's cotton pads, to continue looking for a sport coat, in fact, too fatigued, he thought, especially in light of the previous days' exertions, not to mention the nocturnal indigestion he had suffered after his overlarge meal, to do anything other than go back to his apartment and lie down, and he likely would have done just that had he not passed a small vintage clothing store, in the front window of which hung a worn, but nevertheless appealing brown velvet sport coat, which looked like it might fit him, a supposition that proved, happy event, to be accurate, and so pleased was Harry by this bit of luck, that he let the young woman helping him convince him that he should acquire a stack of green, blue, orange, and red T-shirts, each with a different image emblazoned on its chest, to wear under it, that this was the sort of thing that was fashionable in many cities, for men of all ages who cared about their appearance, as were thin-soled high-top sneakers with red stripes—"suitable, outside the urban context, for wrestling"—a gently used pair of which she slipped onto Harry's feet and, a moment later, collected his money for, while simultaneously and courteously dropping his windbreaker and short-sleeved polyester button-up shirt in the garbage and handing him an indigo silk scarf, "on the house," that a customer she didn't like had left behind several days before, so that when after getting directions to a café where he might gently celebrate his purchases Harry took his leave, he found that his fatigue had left him, and that there was even a certain amount of spring to his step as he moved across the variegated grays of the sidewalk in his new shoes.

A T THE CAFÉ—WHICH AS IT TURNED OUT WAS JUST AROUND
the corner from his apartment—Harry ordered a
sparkling water and a packet of chips and stood at the
counter and felt agreeably, in his deep blue scarf, red T-
shirt, and brown velvet jacket, and with the evening paper
he had picked up along the way, like the rather crisp echo
of some supporting actor from a New Wave film that no
one had ever seen because the studio had lost its funding
and the film had been left to molder in a warehouse and
the director had died and the producer had never liked the
project, which had stolen too much from Godard and not
enough from Truffaut, even as it thumbed its nose at
Rohmer and embraced Varda, etc., and Harry kept going
with this for quite some time, so long, in fact, that he had
finished drink and chips both and was beginning to explore
nuances of the general plot line—he had promoted himself
to co-star status and had made himself the architect of a
scheme to steal the bells of a provincial cathedral through
machinations involving a secretary working in the mayor's
office who had a frog fetish and kept posters of endangered
tree frogs around her workspace (in short, just the sort of
somewhat moving, slightly somber, brilliantly stupid content out of which the New Wave engineered its complexi-
ties)—all the while looking from time to time at himself in
the mirror behind the bar in a state of wonder at what he
found himself calling "his inexplicable frivolity," and while

in the main he liked what he saw in the only very subtly warped glass, he had to admit that the overall impression, scarf and jacket and happy thoughts or not, was one of dilapidation, which he didn't like to think of being set down on film for the consideration of anyone, especially when that anyone might mean viewers in the future, who would almost certainly find Harry and everyone around him horribly old-fashioned, unwashed, and half-diseased, in the way that one age naturally looks back in pity and horror, far more frequently than in admiration, at the paradigms of the other, particularly as preserved in celluloid and/or digital media, in other words, "putting myself down for the record would be a problematic venture at best," Harry thought with a sigh, just as a tall, elegantly dressed man with extraordinary turquoise eyes and cheekbones that looked as if they could break razors came and stood beside him and ordered a sparkling water, then after a moment coughed and bowed and introduced himself as Ireneo.

"MY NAME IS HARRY," HARRY SAID, THEN CALLED FOR another sparkling water and a second packet of chips, while registering that Ireneo's face was so striking and his eyes so unusually colored that it was going to be mildly difficult to look at him as they conversed, which is what he sensed was going to occur at any moment— Ireneo's arrival and rather formal introduction, not to mention how politely but firmly he made it clear that he was going to have no reciprocal trouble looking at Harry, seeming to presage this—but minutes were elapsing, and sips of sparkling water were being taken both by him and by Ireneo, who had a pleasant way of holding his glass with one hand and more or less cupping it with the other, all the while fixing Harry with his turquoise eyes, something Harry might ordinarily by now have found unsettling, but despite his misgivings he was still half-inhabiting his cinematic adventure and imagining he was someone else, and although he knew the shoe that had hung suspended since he had stepped into the vintage clothing store would drop at any moment and he would experience the crushing sense of fatigue and hopelessness that would drive him back to his bed to begin a horrible night, in which, nifty new bell or no nifty new bell, his sleeplessness and exhaustion would do their grim tango and jab at him with their sharpened heels, for the moment he felt almost jaunty, and the café and Ireneo and an unusually handsome woman with flecks of silver paint on her face and wrists sitting alone in the window, not to mention the moment of relative lightness he was experiencing, seemed an agreeable matrix of potential and mystery, so he sipped his water and ate his chips and waited for the conversation to begin, but when Ireneo did speak it was not to begin a conversation, it was to say, "Please come with me."

A T THAT VERY MOMENT, THE CEILING OPENED UP AND THE
heavy shoe Harry had been waiting for fell, grazed his
shoulder, and landed with a loud whamp beside him, and
something all-too-familiar took up its station on his back
and dipped its claws into his shoulders and the most ten-
der parts of his kidneys, and his knees almost buckled, and
he knew his bed and darkened room, and perhaps the new
bell, were the only answer, but there he was standing in the
bright light holding a packet of chips with Ireneo looking
on, so he found his voice and said that he was indisposed
and would have to offer his regrets—he actually used the
word "regrets"—but perhaps another night, whereupon,
with Ireneo still looking at him, he settled his bill, did his
best to finish his water and, though he wasn't sure why,
gave the bright orange packet of chips a pat on its crinkly
flank and walked out through the double glass doors into
the dark, where the puddles of light leaking out of the half-
lit shops made him think of a dream he had once had in
which he was caught in a flooding aquarium, and as Harry
wrapped himself in such thoughts and hurried home,
Ireneo held his position, and slowly finished his water,
although his eyes flicked across the room for a moment to
the handsome, silver-flecked woman sitting alone at her
table and as he did so his brow furrowed, and he took his
hand off his glass, pressed his fingers into the bar and wondered whether he had gotten things right, and while the

woman did not bring her eyes over quickly enough to meet his, she did feel his gaze and did look up at him, before returning to her newspaper and a story about a forensic entomologist who in her spare moments taught children to paint with maggots, which she was reading as the flimsiest of covers for her own melancholy.

B Y THIS TIME, HARRY WAS MORE THAN HALFWAY HOME AND, to his surprise, was beginning to feel somewhat better, the thing on his back had retracted its claws, and his breathing had deepened and he was looking with actual relish—rather than grim resignation—upon the prospect of once again locking his door behind him and lying down to begin the night with a cool towel over his eyes and listening to the small array of sounds haunting his walls and floor and ceiling, adding to them with his new bell, while he mulled over his odd, abrogated interaction with Ireneo, which he registered was an indication, this "willing contemplation of potential interaction," as a counselor had put it more than once, that the crisis he was currently undergoing was a minor one, and not, after all, the kind that so often left him incapacitated, his breath reduced to a sort of peripatetic bubbling associated with heavy porridge and cold bogs, when from a distance he saw Señora Rubinski, his downstairs neighbor, standing outside the door to their apartment building, waiting for her husband to appear and collect her for their evening stroll, even though this husband was long-dead, something she did frequently, unpredictably, and with the greatest sociability—Harry had twice already found himself trapped in conversation—so that it was clear to our hero, in no mood to interact, that he had no choice but to turn on his heel and hurry back the way he had come, a maneuver he executed with just a touch of theatricality, vaguely hoping that if Señora Rubinski had caught sight of him turning around she would imagine that he had forgotten something and had to go back, which happened all the time, etc., *Ha ha!* what a fool he was, he thought, and went striding back the way he had come, moving even faster than he had previously, since he was meant to be rushing back to recuperate some lost item or relate some important information, and hurrying was a relative phenomenon, so that before very long he found himself passing the café and the very window the paint-speckled woman was still sitting in, and although she did not notice him, he found himself struck by her again, in fact, more than struck: smacked, which was perhaps the most remarkable of the many fresh sensations he had experienced that evening, but he pressed on, did not break stride, even ducked his head, suddenly fearful that Ireneo might see him and become confused and perhaps offended, and he thought about this unfortunate possibility, of offending Ireneo, with such vigor that upon rounding the corner and beginning to put distance between himself and the violet glow of the café, and the light spilling out of the half-lit shops, he did not notice the elegant shadow languidly cutting the dark stretch of street before him, until he had come abreast of it, and Ireneo smiled and took his arm and said, "I'm glad you've changed your mind, Harry, yes, I'm very glad."

"I'M VERY GLAD TOO," HARRY SAID, HARDLY MEANING IT, AND as he walked along beside Ireneo, he found himself thinking with longing of being caught for a few minutes in Señora Rubinski's web, of listening to her and nodding and contributing the odd syllable here and there, of admiring the photograph of her husband she liked to take out of a purple silk wrapping she had put around it and show people, and then, at an appropriate moment, of stepping past her and into the entryway of his building and beginning to climb the creaking stairs in his new shoes, but instead, here he was: chilled, out of breath, and more than a little sick to his stomach, negotiating one markedly empty street after another with this Ireneo, who still hadn't said where they were going and had nothing to recommend him besides his eyes, cheekbones, and pleasant way of drinking sparkling water, and yet he, Harry, kept walking and even blurted, as if to affirm how happy he was at this turn of events, that the bags he was carrying were the result of a shopping expedition he had undertaken that afternoon, a particularly inane remark that Ireneo countered with unadulterated silence, which did not prevent Harry from following up with the observation, in an instance of "over-sharing" if ever there was one, that he suffered from a profound sleep disorder to do with his legs, one that affected some five percent of the world's population and made sustained mental and physical activity indispensable if he was to relax enough to sleep, although this time Ireneo turned and looked at him, unblinking, for several seconds, before saying, politely but noncommittally, "I see,"

"I've just tried acupuncture in an attempt to deal with it as well as other problems,"

"And did you find it effective?"

"I just went the once, yesterday,"

"Ah,"

"Then I bought a bell,"

"A bell,"

"The kind you ring at hotels and doctor's offices if you need help,"

"I see,"

so that the upshot of Harry's attempts at drawing out his companion was that he felt slightly worse than he had before he had spoken, but even when Ireneo at last held open a green carriage door that gave onto a cobblestone courtyard at the end of which Harry perceived a large, dimly lit window filled with unmoving people dressed in somber colors, standing with their backs to him, which Ireneo announced as their destination, so far was Harry from mounting any resistance that he momentarily took the lead as they crossed the courtyard and went in through a small door next to the large window and joined the crowd of, yes, very nearly unmoving people, who were dressed entirely in something akin to mourning, so that Harry, in looking at their backs and shoulders, felt his eyes falling into familiar chasms, black openings in the dim air, which felt to him chillingly consummated mere moments after Ireneo had shut the door behind them, when he heard a click and the room was plunged into a darkness that seemed to explode out of the black clothing and that remained unmitigated long after it seemed to Harry that his eyes should have adjusted to it.

HARRY WAS NO STRANGER TO LIGHTLESS CHAMBERS, IN FACT for whole months he had spent his free time, i.e, the hours not passed in his gray bedroom or in his slowly decomposing cubicle at work, in a chair placed dead-center in a windowless room in the basement of his former house, where he had unscrewed the lightbulb and would sit, hoping that in the miasma of black he had created the conditions would be right—though right for what he wasn't certain: some shift, some alteration, perhaps some new dispensation that would allow him to walk out of this world and into some other—but after a time he had begun to find himself troubled by the blackness, the mockery it made of his eyes, the sounds it seemed to heighten, small scratching noises, bits of breathing he couldn't trace, tufts of cold air on his ear or toe, and he had begun avoiding the windowless room, indeed had long ago left the chair sitting there and locked it up, like he had now done with his entire house, forever, which is what he began to wish he could do here, even though he had only just arrived, and while he was thinking this and other things, an old woman wearing what appeared to be an illuminated lampshade on her head appeared in the depths of the room and began walking toward him, and it struck Harry that the crowd that had been there must have dispersed, because her path toward him was unimpeded, and before he could take a precautionary step backwards she was standing in front of him with her eyes shut, permanently or not he could not have said, as the light cast by the lampshade or whatever was in it was imperfect at best, but this didn't matter because then the woman began humming, something vaguely incantatory, and as she did so her lampshade went off and lampshades began to flicker around the edges of the room, where the people had apparently positioned themselves, causing their faces to float for a moment like ruined petals, Harry thought, amidst the blackness, with the effect that he began to feel as if he were floating just a little along with them, so that when the old woman stopped humming and said, "Now I will tell you what it is you have come to hear," Harry heard it from on high, as it were, and answered more loudly than perhaps the situation merited, although he understood quickly enough that this was not what caused the old woman to throw open her eyes, quickly look him over, then yell, "Lights out!" whereupon she vanished leaving a globular afterimage that danced before Harry's eyes long after Ireneo had hustled him back out of the doors they had come in through and out onto the street, where, as the pale yellow thing still bobbed before him, Ireneo gesticulated and rolled his turquoise eyes and said, "It was her, I knew it, I should have known it, they told me to bring the one with the broken face, it was her," and for a moment they both, Harry thought, looked into the yellow globe before them and saw the handsome woman from the café sitting cross-legged inside it, flecks of silver sparkling like tinfoil on her face, which didn't stop him from saying to Ireneo, "Who, who was her?" and Ireneo from bowing, apologizing, turning on his heel, and walking away.

HARRY FOUND SO APPEALING THE IDEA THAT HIS sparklingly clean but manifestly still-broken face had led Ireneo to mistakenly summon him instead of the silver woman to the ceremony of the lamps, as he called her and it as he lay in bed fighting his legs later that night and then the next morning over tea and miniature pastries, that, after trying and failing several times to find the mysterious house again, he began doubling up on his appearances at the café in hopes of encountering either her or Ireneo, but the world had swerved away from or swallowed that trajectory, and he saw neither of them, and no one he spoke to at the counter of the bar could call to mind the tall man with the turquoise eyes or the woman with the flecks of silver on her face, and by and by he again found himself beating hasty retreats to his bed, ringing his bell, dodging or not dodging Señora Rubinski, murmuring greetings to his neighbors and wandering the streets of the city or sitting on one of its wide beaches or stumbling around its often oddly shaped plazas, which were invariably constructed around statues and/or fountains: focal points for the eye that might otherwise have been pulled away into the shadows that held sway along the jagged periphery, thought Harry, one day when he was feeling particularly susceptible to what he called the loathsome generalities, abstractions like "everyone" and "everything," that crushed whatever came in their way, whether it was the everyone associated with the office, the everyone who announced that the period for grieving had long since expired and that it was high time for one to get off one's sorry ass and come back to the cubicle, as it were, or the everything associated with the stars and moon, the earth and oceans, the red sandstone yawing in monstrous slabs out of the calm green slopes, the snow that covered, froze, and quieted it all, the world, in short, that entered through your burning eyes and bludgeoned your sorry soul—*So much that cuts our legs out from under us*—"I couldn't agree more," said a man just after Harry had thought this, as he stood beneath a striped green awning that looked out through a bright drizzle over a fringe of evergreen bushes to a monument to some group or other of the once-honored dead, and although the man was speaking to the woman next to him and not to Harry, Harry looked in his direction and thought, *You're just saying that,* and without missing the proverbial beat the man said, "Quite the contrary, I might have said the same thing myself and in just those words,"

I have a recurring dream, thought Harry,

"Oh really?" said the man,

This awning is reminding me of it,

"Go on,"

A ship takes me to a distant city, we arrive at night, I am meant to disembark with a group for a tour of some sort, but I disembark alone and am quickly lost in winding streets,

"A labyrinth,"

Of sorts, only before long it resolves itself and I am in the very bazaar the group had been meant to visit: an agreeable affair next to a long canal, with stalls of blue and violet glassware mixed in with piles of bolts, bicycle chains, jewelry boxes, all backlit by lamps that set the glassware alight,

"That must have made for a beautiful reflection in the water,"

Yes, and in fact before long I am on the canal, shopping at the reflected stalls, which are tended by children,

"Children?"

Which is odd because there was no one tending the stalls above the surface,

"That is odd,"

I want to buy something, but can't decide what to buy,

"Too many choices?"

Everything is too lovely, and all this loveliness, which emanates in equal part from the glowing wares and the children's faces, short-circuits my ability to think, and I just stand there without being able to move,

"You've lost something,"

But in the dream I can't think of what it is, all I can do is stand there, without moving, as the dark from the water slowly gains the upper hand on the light from the stalls, and all around me people are streaming back toward the harbor, where the ship is waiting to leave, but I don't leave, I just stand there, which is what Harry did, for quite some time after the man and his companion had left, and the rain had stopped falling, and the pigeons and green parrots, which sometimes flew with them, had returned to preen and dry their feathers in the sun that was now coating the monument to the dead, dripping off all of its exposed surfaces, burning off the rainwater gathered there between the surrounding cobblestones.

WHEN HARRY FINALLY COLLECTED HIMSELF AND LEFT, HE felt that by telling someone about his dream he had gotten something essential off his chest, something that had had to be removed, like the mineral scale that, unaddressed, builds up in small, water-reliant appliances like espresso machines and warm-air humidifiers, eventually choking them, and as he continued his explorations it seemed like the sprawling city, which nevertheless remained wrapped in a veil of mystery that he was certain his multiple incursions would do little to mitigate, was in some way opening to him, and that his knotted mind was at last untying itself, with the happy result that when one afternoon, upon visiting one of the city's many spectacular museums, where bits of the distant past had been hammered up on the wall alongside multilingual explanatory notices, he had great difficulty deciphering what was being proposed about the glistening armor hanging before him, a fact he found more curious than troubling, and he was even encouraged, rather than perturbed, to note that this moment of ocular aphasia before the explanatory notice reminded him that in the old days he had often woken not so much not knowing where he was, but not knowing who it was he was lying next to, which had more than once made him leap up and grab for his pants, afraid that his then-wife, upon waking, would be horrified to find a total stranger lying nearly naked beside her, and that when that dynamic had ceased being possible, i.e. when the bed beside him had become empty, he had more than once woken with the sensation that the emptiness beside him would at any moment awake and, seeing him lying on the bed partially clad, scream, and that scream would destroy him, so he had started sleeping on the couch and had not stopped sleeping on the couch until he had arrived in this new city, where he had a single bed, a sequence of thought that had continued to attend but not disturb him as he left the museum and drifted back down to the city from the heights where it was located, to which layers—upon layers—of mental fog he attributed his inability to recognize the handsome woman from the café when, less than an hour after he had stood gazing without comprehension at the three-by-three-inch sign, he stood gazing without comprehension at her.

A FTERWARDS, HARRY REALIZED THAT HE HAD MORE THAN once walked past her, that she had been hidden in plain sight, like the letter in the famous Edgar Allan Poe story, which mechanism had baffled all attempts to find it because it lay out in the open where everyone could see it and so, in the natural order of things, didn't, a comparison he liked quite a good deal even though the two ends didn't quite match up—she after all had neither been hidden nor was hiding—and which prompted him, some weeks later, when it was all over, to seek out the story in question and reread it over a plate of sliced quince and tuna wedges and a glass of sparkling water at a small specialty shop near the market, out of which he had emerged when he stepped onto the broad sloping central pedestrian boulevard that split the city and led down to the sea, and which he had walked along nearly every day, remarking, assuredly, upon the numerous "living statues" who had set up their more or less elaborate shop along the edges, to the general delight of tourists and to the more specific delight, as Harry was unfortunately to learn, of certain local connoisseurs, though never before having stopped in front of one, as he did shortly after starting down the street on this day, in front of this extraordinary silver angel, with her enormous silver wings and beautiful silver face, down one cheek of which coursed frozen, silver tears, upon which Harry gazed with wonder then sudden, spine-stiffening recognition that grabbed him up and shoved him through to the front of the small crowd surrounding her, whose members were snapping pictures and remarking on the elaborateness of her costume, really one of the best, so much more marvelous than the fairly predictable Che Guevara, or the chubby Julius Caesar, or the man with his own head on a plate, or the creaky, battling robots, or the lady dressed as a fruit stand: this was on a par with the golden centaur, or the two platinum men on bicycles, a real work of art, *Yes, a work of art,* thought Harry, who stood on the sidewalk no more than three feet away from the silver box the angel seemed bolted to and gazed up into her hardly blinking eyes, which did not move even when she very precisely arched her back, then lifted a shoulder, then twisted her arm, and after a few minutes he was asked by several of the onlookers to step aside, there were pictures to be taken, he was blocking the full view, in short, "What the fuck, man?" but Harry did not move, kept gazing up into her eyes, even as the murmuring around him grew louder, less relaxed, until suddenly it struck him that she was, perhaps because of him, on the verge of breaking her silence, that by standing there and somewhat impudently staring at her, he was committing a transgression, interfering with her act, possibly even making her nervous, which was exactly the opposite of his intent: he had thought long and hard on this, the two of them with their broken faces could eat together, share a drink, take a stroll, apply tape and glue to each other, but now he could see that the situation would require much more than a casual "Hi, they thought I was you," and that his standing in front of her, in all her splendor, like a troll lying in ambush beneath a handsome bridge, was no way to get things started, so he bowed his head and, with the idea of in some way mitigating the disturbance he had caused, murmured an apology then backed away slowly, rather ridiculously, before turning and moving off down the boulevard, where eventually he passed Julius Caesar, then a rather good Atlas with golden dreadlocks, who had set down his globe and was sweeping the ground in front of his box, and then Che Guevara, who had a plastic cigar stuffed in his mouth and was engaged in lighting and throwing tiny firecrackers onto the ground.

CHEEKS BURNING AS HE HURRIED AWAY, HARRY REMINDED himself that, in his defense, he had stumbled upon the silver angel by accident, and that while it was true that this accident had occurred in the context of his attempts to locate her, it was still an accident, that could not be disputed, or could it? hmmm . . . : he had been looking for her and had found her, and hadn't his method been more or less to stagger around the city until their paths crossed again? and hadn't that been what had happened? it had, but, still, in what sense had he, actually, been looking for her? wasn't he mistaking what had been reduced to rather a wan hope, one stripped of all but the most desultory agency, with active engagement? wouldn't any outside, so-called impartial observer briefed on the situation exclaim, "but you weren't looking for her, you were just flopping around, you may have been thinking about her in some abstract way as you went out, but that's pretty far from constituting a search"? but what constitutes a search? Harry wondered, what is the cut-off point? the point beyond which the activity ceases to be what we have mistaken it for? once, over coffee, a well-meaning friend had put her hand on his shoulder and said, "what are you doing? that was years ago, years and years . . ." and he had taken a sip of his coffee and said, "I'm searching"—in much the same tone, he realized as he passed a pair of living tree statues, fairly nice ones, that he had used in making his comment to the pigeon about beginning his "assault on life" and his comment to the man under the awning about the number of hurdles life lines up before you—but what, exactly, had he meant by that? had he been describing an open-ended engagement, one that, perhaps, continued even now? this seemed plausible, and rather interesting, insofar as said search could be seen as an umbrella for the search he had or had not been conducting for the woman he had or had not found, but which was it? had he, in this subsidiary instance, been searching or hadn't he? could he, in other words, fairly attribute a portion of his boorish behavior in front of the angel to his astonishment at having found—rather than stumbled across—her? and what (the fuck, he thought) was the difference? it was hard to say, which was the way so many of his arguments with himself ended: in depressing stalemates, he far and away preferred losing to himself, as at least in those instances he achieved some approximation of clarity, and clarity, even the false variety, was inarguably something, etc., Harry thought, and as he did so, moving all the way down the long avenue and toward the water, the handsome woman, the woman with paint on her face, the silver angel—whose name, it is time for her to have one, was Solange—stood on her box, and thought not about Harry, whom she had barely noticed and had quickly forgotten, but about a path lit by star- and moonlight, one she had heard the dead were obliged to travel before leaving this sphere, and that for some was very long and for others very short, and she wanted to know which, in the case of her lost one, it was, and not knowing was troubling her and preventing her, and her lost one, she suspected, from moving on, which was why when, a week ago, after she had found the little salmon-colored slip of paper on the subway platform that guaranteed answers to "insoluble questions," she had telephoned the number given and had been told to wait at the café where we first encountered her and where Ireneo made his mistake.

FOR HIS PART, IRENEO, WHO HAD QUICKLY SHRUGGED OFF ANY sense of guilt about having brought Harry along to the "answer session" at his employer's apartment, due to the inherent, not to mention typical, vagaries of his brief—"Bring me the one with the broken face"—had in fact been tasked with finding the woman, but quickly realizing what to Harry would seem so problematic—that only serendipity would bring him back into contact with her, who in arranging to be present at the café at the given hour had communicated neither name nor number—he had done exactly nothing besides keep his turquoise eyes open as he went about his business, which in the vicinity of the moment we have lately been considering, had him lighting candles for the dead at a church no more than a quarter mile away from where Solange stood unhappy, unmoving, on her silver box, and less than that from the living tree statues that Harry passed on his way down the boulevard, a relative proximity that all three of them, had they known, would in the light of their later association have found bracing, Ireneo no less than Harry and Solange, still, what is most pertinent at the moment is that among the seventeen red candles Ireneo had been tasked with lighting by his employer Doña Eulalia—the old woman who had spoken to Harry while intending to speak to Solange—three related to the former and one to the latter, and as soon as they were lit, this very Doña Eulalia, who was sitting quite some distance away on a small red sofa by the window of her bedroom, felt a sharp urge to sit up straight and take a deep breath and insert a mint-lemon drop into her mouth, only the last of which she did, while thinking, "I should have spoken to him while he was here, and now where is he, and more importantly, who are *they*? for even though *something* had come across authoritatively enough to her in the days following Harry's unexpected appearance for her to expand the list of souls she was actively tracking, she didn't know who the candles that corresponded to Harry were, any more than she knew who the single candle was that corresponded to Solange, though there were things of course that she could say about them: saying things, however imprecise, about the souls corresponding to the candles she was forever sending Ireneo off to light was her business, though there were times—like now as she sat on the sofa sucking on her mint-lemon drop wishing she could tell Ireneo where, for example, to find both Harry and Solange, which would simplify things considerably—she wished she were better at it,

"I wish I were better at it," she said aloud,

"But I'm not and to bloody hell with it," she added,

a sentiment she softened by appending an "ah well," which turned out to be one of those moments of synchronicity that, in the so-called grand scheme of things, are far more common than we suspect and than we may soon choose to believe, for at precisely the moment she emitted her "ah well," Ireneo in front of his candles, Solange (though she said it silently) on her silver box and Harry who was just stepping onto the beach, said "ah well" along with her, and their reasons for saying it were not so terribly different.

THAT MORNING, ON HIS WAY OUT TO SEARCH OR WANDER, whichever, Harry had stopped off in a bookstore, browsed a few minutes, then, without thinking much about it, had purchased a slender red volume in a language he no longer knew terribly well, had slipped it, still in its crisp paper bag, into the pocket of his brown velvet jacket, where he could feel it pressing lightly against his ribs, then pulled it out again and read some of it in a sprawling bed of daffodils outside one of the museums he would later visit—and where he would have such a strange time with the explanatory notice—the story, as best he could parse it, of a man who sometime in the middle ages, when Christianity has ostensibly swept Europe clean of its shadows, encounters the Greek god Pan, now much reduced and mud-covered, in the salty marshes of the South of France, but who appears to him, even "so long after he might most fully have mattered," like some "dread avatar of forgotten impulses," and now, just after joining Solange, Ireneo, and Doña Eulalia in half-murmuring, "ah well," Harry sat down on the crowded—it was a lovely afternoon with just the lightest bit of breeze and a glorious warmth to the sand—beach, spent a few moments looking out through the fat palm trees over the gaily colored umbrellas to the ship-speckled horizon and the deep seam where sky and sea did their endless, distant dance, a place his father had long ago convinced him was full of wonders—ships made out of water, fish made out of air, only, of course, try as you might, you could never get there, and although his father might well have used this evocation as the basis for a paternal lesson in the unattainable aspects of life, he never had, for which Harry found himself suddenly quite grateful: what a load of crap such lessons were: life always had the upper hand, no matter how many little stories you told yourself about it—then pulled the book out of his pocket, opened it, found his visual aphasia had again returned, but, this time, along with it, a sense that some forgotten impulse he had been harboring, along with his heart, in the pit of his stomach, was staggering out into the light—perhaps set free, in the first instance, by the change of locale, and, in the second, by a combination of the acupuncture treatment, the purchase of the bell, the adventure with Ireneo, and the conversation with the man under the awning, not to mention the stunning particularities of the silver angel herself—and would emerge at any moment, after all these years, and that he should be prepared to step forward, for better or worse, along with it, which thought made him feel giddy and jaunty—like the character in the movie he had imagined— but also completely terrified—what tack to take?—so that after staring a moment longer into the deep seam of the horizon and imagining he was on the verge of reaching that impossible place where he could float alongside hybrid marvels of sky and sea, or at least dream up some way to inoffensively approach the silver angel, some way that wouldn't result in his instant and definitive dismissal, he ran back home, closed the shutters, and jumped into bed.

TWO DAYS LATER, HARRY OPENED THEM AGAIN WITH A PLAN, or rather the bright beginnings of one, and while, after so recently spending so much time on the inside of his head, one might expect that a good deal of slightly soggy thinking had gone into reaching it—a long-ago colleague, subjected to a lengthy dose of Harry's thought process, once compared it to the higgledy-piggledy fretwork of boards laid down in pre-modern times across bogs and marshes, the remains of which could still be found, along with the victims of their treachery, in certain regions of Europe—on this occasion, Harry had simply woken, legs still twitching, with a bucket of golden paint floating before his eyes, so that after he had spent a bit of time with the local yellow pages, executed his ablutions, and made a lightning dash, back pressed against the side of the building, behind and past Señora Rubinski, who was standing outside the door tapping her foot, he paid a visit to Almundo's Store for Living Statues, which he had selected as much for the size of its advertisement—twice that of Ernesto's Living Statue Emporium—as for its proximity to his apartment, nor was he disappointed, as Almundo was able with great efficiency and appealing panache to kit Harry out with everything—including gilded armor, gilded box, gilded lance, golden body paint, body-paint remover, a large duffel bag—he would need to make a most convincing living statue, one that would,

51 :: RAY OF THE STAR

according to Almundo, attract the greatest sympathy of passersby and provide the foundation upon which he could transmit the full flourishing of his artistry,

"Speaking of which," Harry said, "any suggestions?"

"Stand very still, my friend," said Almundo, "stand very, very still,"

"And beyond that?" Harry asked,

"Look down, think happy thoughts, and bathe every evening to keep your skin from breaking out," said Almundo,

"Thank you, I will," said Harry, eager to get started, but already dusk was sweeping through the city, lights were flicking on, and as he alternated between hefting and dragging his duffel bag, it became clearer and clearer that he would have to wait until the next day to make his debut, which did not stop him, once he had done a medium-length tour of duty with Señora Rubinski, from spending a quiet hour on his box in front of the wall mirror in his bedroom, dressed and made up as what had been pitched to him by Almundo as the one and only "Knight of the Woeful Countenance," but which, at least in the problematic light of his floor lamp, made him look dangerously like some kind of laminated hobgoblin or gigantic duck.

STILL, HE ROSE VERY EARLY THE NEXT MORNING, ATE SOME hard sausage and a tomato, drank half a bottle of sparkling water, applied his makeup, packed his duffel bag, and made his way to the slowly waking boulevard where he set himself up in what he recalled being a largish gap in the line of statues—of which there were none yet in sight, it being far too early—at a point he decided was more or less equidistant between the golden centaur and a large flower kiosk, and had the advantage of being situated directly beneath one of the largest plane trees on the boulevard, which, during the heat of the day, would provide him with some measure of shade, and then, with a steady stream of locals on their way to work and a few sleepy tourists heading for fresh juice, melons, packets of nuts, and glass cups of milky coffee at the market drifting past him, he planted his golden box, pulled on his golden costume, did a few preemptive deep knee bends and arm stretches, swiped at the air with his lance, then stepped up and struck an overly elaborate pose—a sort of supplicant's arrangement he had puzzled out the previous evening in front of the mirror in lieu of his normal anti-RLS routine— which he held for what seemed like ages, but was really more like three minutes, and then tried another, and another, and so began a very long day, one that, by the by, involved assorted insults, copious sweating, a cornucopia of low-grade pains, far too much thinking about the folly of human endeavor generally and his own specifically, and a patent inability not to forget that he was meant to be a statue of sorts and crane his neck in order to catch a glimpse of the silver angel, who, when in the early afternoon she appeared one hundred meters up from him, he could just see shining off in the distance like a silver suffix to all that had gone wrong in his life and a silver prefix to all that might, if he could only—fat chance—hold his position long enough, and, over time, move his box far enough up the boulevard, still go right.

WHILE HARRY STOOD, WOEFUL, LET'S FACE IT, INDEED, ON his box under the giant plane tree, already well aware—even with downcast eyes one could both see and of course hear the snickering—that the passersby, when they arrived at the silver angel, would now include him along with the other second and third raters in their commentary when they stood in wonder before her beautiful, broken face and extraordinary wings, Solange stood on her own box thinking about the little salmon-colored slip of paper with the number she now realized—having gotten over the sense of desperation that had set in after no one had arrived that evening in the café to collect her—she very much wished to redial, while being cognizant that upon returning home after having been, so to speak, stood up in what had felt like her hour of greatest need, instead of covering it in the Lucite she had on hand and that she used almost daily on certain objects in a largely unarticulated attempt to afford them some measure of permanence or protection, she had torn it to shreds and thrown it out the window and watched it float down through leaves and lights toward the street below her building, and that although for days she had combed the ground inside and out of the subway she had not found a replacement, only gum wrappers, beer bottle labels, shopping lists, burned photographs, bits of plastic and endless shards of shattered colored glass, the whole, it seemed to her, threatening to rise as if caught in fierce winds and blot out whatever dim light she was still able to shine on the calming songs she had always sung to herself: in short, still not so good and maybe even a little worse, the mental state of Solange, the silver angel, and it was certainly untainted by any awareness that a woeful knight/laminated hobgoblin/my God, what the fuck are you supposed to be, friend? had set up his shop down the boulevard in hopes of eventually edging his way into her peripheral and maybe, eventually, frontal vision: how strange the storms, some small, some large, that are forever sweeping over us before we've even had a chance to think "I must seek shelter," and Ireneo, meanwhile, had taken up jogging.

REDISCOVERED JOGGING MIGHT BE MORE ACCURATE IN THIS instance, as Ireneo had once done a very good deal of jogging indeed, so much so that at university, when he was still "on track" to take a degree in contemporary finance and assume a position in his mother's accounting firm, which would have given him, even at the entry level, access to a company car and a company apartment and an expense account pointed skyward—in other words "the works"—he had been a member of the school running club, and had often finished near the head of the pack when informal races were organized, but that had been long ago, so long in fact that when, after Doña Eulalia had asked him to step up his efforts to find Harry and Solange, and he had thought of how much more distance he could cover at a run, he was no longer aware that he still owned a pair of beat-up but serviceable Asics running shoes, so that their apparent apparition—he had set them there, in the guise of bookends, so long ago that they had ceased, in any meaning-ful way, to exist—on either end of the mantel over the blocked-up fireplace in his modest studio, with their shoelaces intact but wildly akimbo, read to him as an extispicic instance whose meaning would only become clear after he had laced up the shoes and used them to put an end to his search, so after digging out a pair of cotton socks, he had pulled them on, taken a long pull on a bottle of sparkling water, and run out his front door, into the city, where although obviously he had done nothing in the way of training in years, he had found that, even in slacks and rather a tight linen shirt, he could run without pause for hour upon hour, as if his feet were enchanted, the thought of which prompted the slightest of smiles to infiltrate his otherwise impassive features, happy occurrence that lit his turquoise eyes and further lifted his cheekbones, so that it would have been hard to say whether all the men and women who looked at him as he ran past were doing so because he was loping along in his street clothes or because he was so striking, which of course is neither here nor there, except that eyes and faces flipped in his direction as if pulled sharply by a string and for a time Ireneo found this distracting and worried that all the attention he was receiving would negatively impact on his ability to search, but just as he was thinking this it seemed to him that his old shoes began whispering to him—*turn left at the next corner, run as close as you can to the beautiful display of antique toy cars in that shop window, nod at the construction worker who is having trouble negotiating that alley with his untrustworthy backhoe, sprint across the chalk-colored museum courtyard where the skateboarders hold sway, cut through the market but don't run or barely run and make sure to lift and sniff a melon or a papaya as you go, hum a little, jog above the sea and take in deep gulps of the fresh air, take a turn down the boulevard*—and he liked the sound of this whispering, which kept him company even as, at stoplights, he was obliged to run in place, though he also found it moderately unsettling and decided to ask Doña Eulalia what she thought about it, when after he completed his search he saw her next, which, he had a feeling, now that he had rediscovered these marvelous shoes, wouldn't—just as Doña Eulalia had predicted—be long.

THAT BOTH DOÑA EULALIA AND IRENEO PROVED TO BE wrong—in the short term because Ireneo's old Asics, for reasons all their own, instructed him to keep his head pointed pavementward on the boulevard; in the slightly longer term because Ireneo's mother, who now lived in elegant retirement up the coast, fell gravely ill and required his immediate attendance—was far from unfortunate in re the potential of an eventual dynamic unfolding between the silver angel and the Knight of the Woeful Countenance, not least because the information that Doña Eulalia was ever more eager to provide them most likely would have, had it been imparted too early, especially the portion concerning Harry and the candles, had a chilling effect, difficult to overcome, even on considerably more solid ground than that provided by a gold box moving (even only in potential—Harry didn't yet think he was ready) toward a silver box (which had no idea said gold box was coming), on the crowded matrix of a pedestrian thoroughfare so bustling, so full, as they say, of life and its attendant distractions, and detractors/detractions, such as the three old men who, just as Harry, four days into his self-imposed calvary, was beginning, in great earnest, to consider packing it in for the afternoon, came and stood before him, folded their arms over their chests, and launched into a withering appraisal of Harry's utter lack not just of artistry, but also of even the smallest degree of presence, to the point, as they put it, that he was almost invisible,

"Yes practically invisible," one of them said,

"I can't believe we noticed him,"

"But of course we did,"

"In the end,"

"Still, we did see him,"

"He's not invisible enough,"

"This is not a promising debut,"

"Another sorry Don,"

"Just like last year's,"

"Although last year's was better,"

"Marginally, but it's true that silver is better for the Don,"

"The Don must be skinny, this one isn't skinny, I don't say he's fat, but he's certainly not skinny,"

"That's not the worst of it though,"

"No, it's not the worst of it,"

I'm a statue, Harry thought, *I can't move, I can't talk, the bastards, or can I? is this some kind of a test?*

"He should reconsider,"

"I bet he got that getup at Almundo's, the old swindler,"

"We ought to talk to Almundo sometime, pay a visit, it's been a while,"

"His makeup is running,"

"He looks like a giant duck,"

"The Don looked ridiculous, but not like a duck,"

I don't believe this, Harry thought,

"He's hopeless,"

"Won't last the week,"

"Shouldn't last the week,"

"We know you can hear us, friend,"

"Unless he's a foreigner, one who doesn't speak the language,"

"Everyone speaks the language,"

"He looks familiar to me,"

"Everyone looks familiar,"

"That's a long way from being true,"

"It's clear he's listening,"

"The Don wears an old barber bowl for a helmet, that piece of plastic on his head is a poor replica of a real Knight's helmet,"

"And where is the beard and Rosinante for that matter?"

"You can't expect him to have a horse, none of the Dons ever had a horse,"

"But one had a Sancho Panza,"

"That Sancho Panza was little more than a stuffed hippo,"

"Let's go and have some bubbly,"

"With those lovely olives,"

"And a bit of salted cod,"

"He doesn't have the touch,"

"Neither a buffoon nor an artist,"

"Neither here nor there,"

"There's a word for that,"

"The word is 'fucked,'"

Jesus Christ, Harry thought, and after the three old men had uncrossed their arms and gone off to have their goddamn drink and olives, he dropped his lance, shook off his shield, sat down on his box, and fumbled in his duffel bag for a bottle of sparkling water, which to top it all off had come uncapped and was now empty, then looked up the boulevard and saw that, no doubt during his dressing down, the silver angel had vanished, not the first time she had done this while he was not looking, in fact she had managed to do it each day he had come and stood on his box and sweated and been snickered at, *I'm so out of here,* Harry thought, which was when his neighbor, the golden centaur, now free of all but his golden body paint, came and tapped him on the shoulder, shook his hand, introduced himself as Alfonso, and invited him for a drink.

"THEY'RE QUITE RIGHT," SAID ALFONSO ONCE THEY WERE installed in an appealingly deep burgundy booth in the back of a nearby café and had tall, lime-garnished glasses of chilled sparkling water before them, "The connoisseurs are blunt, but they know what they're talking about, as of course they should since they've been monitoring the statues on the boulevard for over fifty years,"

"That long," said Harry,

"I know," said Alfonso,

"But why?"

"It's a pastime like any other, but the point is they always get it right,"

"Has anyone ever ignored them?"

"Of course, but with dire consequences, we're all very loyal to them, as they are to us, once they've decided we merit their attentions,"

"What sort of attentions?"

"A coin or bill here and there to make sure our hats get filled, a bottle of water placed in the shade of our boxes on a hot day, a story to entertain us or make us think when traffic is low or we are or both, a wedge of cheese or sausage when they think we could use it, an antihistamine when a cold or allergy sinks its teeth into us,"

"All that," said Harry,

"And more," said Alfonso, "Once they sent a number of us on a cruise, covered all expenses, draped us, as we embarked, in spangles, pearls, pins, earrings, bracelets, rebates, furs, masks, laces, tiffanies, ruffs, and falls, sent us six hours out to sea where, on an island of verdant lawns and rippling brooks and long, splendid beaches, we were regaled at such great length and so splendidly, by hosts who seemed to intuit our every desire, no matter how sunken below the surface of our external commodities, that we didn't dare sleep for fear of missing even a moment of the happiness that was everywhere to be had, and when we returned we hoisted the connoisseurs high on our shoulders and, cheering, carried them up and down the boulevard until it was time to get back to work,"

"Really?" said Harry,

"More or less," said Alfonso,

"Then it's hopeless,"

"I didn't quite say that, but yes, it is, the boulevard is for serious statues and for serious clowns, again I don't wish to give offense, but you're just a man standing around in a costume, who sweats copiously and moves when he shouldn't, in short you lack the calling,"

"I thought maybe with some practice . . ." said Harry,

"It would take years, it took me years, I went to school for it, basic stuff, juggling invisible apples and getting myself in and out of invisible glass boxes," Alfonso said and made his hands climb backwards up an imaginary flight of steps that ran from the sugar bowl to the mirror above the burgundy seatback behind him, a feat that Harry tried and failed miserably to duplicate,

"No, I don't think so," said Alfonso, not at all unkindly,

"It's just that," said Harry,

"You're hoping to impress someone," said Alfonso,

"A woman, an angel," said Harry,

"Ah, *the* angel," said Alfonso,

"I just want to talk to her,"

"And perhaps get to know her a little and take a walk together and so on,"

"Exactly,"

"Of course, my friend, of course, it's in the nature of things,"

"She and I have something in common,"

"I don't doubt it, and I don't want to make light of your feelings or make fun, but I will permit myself to say that in your admiration for the angel you are neither, as the old expression goes, the first nor will you be the last, though if your goal is to approach and be noticed by her, favorably noticed that is, I'm quite certain your woeful Don Quixote getup won't help you,"

"You're as blunt as the connoisseurs," said Harry,

"Have you attempted to speak to her?"

"Not directly,"

"Wise decision, the last time she returned someone's compliment the results were disastrous,"

"Disastrous?" Harry said, taking a deep sip of his sparkling water and pressing on the wedge of lime with his tongue, the resultant burst of tartness helping to check the momentary feeling of panic that had swept over him when Alfonso had used that word—which word, perhaps for emphasis, perhaps because he had seen and enjoyed the reaction it had caused in Harry, Alfonso used again, then he said,

"Do you have time for another water? if you do I'll tell you a story, about the silver angel and how she came to have those tears on her face,"

"I have time," Harry said,

"It was told to me—as I suspect, since it seems to be common knowledge on the boulevard, it was told to all the others—by the connoisseurs, and I will do my best to use their language and euphemisms in retelling it to you, although of course what you hear will by necessity differ in some hopefully small degree from what they told me,"

"Is what they told you true?" asked Harry,

"True enough, true enough, and if it isn't then at least you will have heard a story, shall we order another round?"

"That will be fine," Harry said.

"ONCE UPON A TIME THERE WAS OR THERE WASN'T A YOUNG woman named Solange who lived in a fine old city by the sea, and each day in that city she painted her face with gold and put on golden robes and wings and went and stood on the boulevard, which is famous the world round for its fine buildings and fine trees and crowds of people, but most of all for its extraordinary living statues, of which Solange, the golden angel, was the most beautiful and the most beloved, for when she smiled the sun slipped out of her mouth and danced in front of the crowds that would gather around her in such numbers that the boulevard was blocked and people seeking passage spilled out onto the surrounding streets, and while young men and young women alike fell hopelessly in love with Solange, and spoke to her and beseeched her to step down off her box, she never answered, never even seemed to look at them, until the day that the sun, having slipped out of her mouth to dance around in the crowd, stopped before a young man, who reached out a long, dusky finger and caressed it, as if it were a cheek, *my cheek,* thought Solange on her golden box, and when a moment later this young man came and stood before her and asked her to step down and join him for a drink, she shocked everyone (the murmur of it, which I remember well, rippled like electric wavelets all the way down the boulevard) by stepping down and removing her wings and walking off with him, and although Solange and the young man were often out and about in the days and weeks that followed it was as if they had pulled on magical cloaks that kept anyone from seeing them clearly, so that when they had been somewhere and then left it was like a dream had come, glowed for a moment, then gone, so love begins, and, in truth, ends, even when it ends so horribly, as Solange's did, one night when her young man had gone out in search of milk and ended his search with a knife blade broken off so far down his throat it took the investigating officials several hours to discover the cause of death, though it did not take them so long to find the one who had broken his knife off in the young man's mouth: after the deed he had drunk a bottle of sparkling water, swallowed a sprig of parsley and a fistful of Valium and went out to inform anyone who would listen that the golden angel, whom he had admired for far longer than the young man, would soon be his and his alone, without knowing that at the precise moment he had shoved his knife blade down the young man's throat the golden angel had ceased to exist, for when, some weeks later, Solange reappeared on the boulevard, she was no longer golden—she had gone as pale as a piece of cloudy ice—and she never smiled, and there were tears on her face, and inside those tears, which she carefully affixed each morning and tore carefully from her face each night, were flecks of the broken blade, which the presiding coroner, who knew her from the boulevard, had given her out of pity, along with a piece of milk-stained cloth, when, after the young man's family had swooped down and swept everything up, she had presented herself and asked in a clear, brittle voice if there was anything left from his final moments that she could have."

WHEN ALFONSO HAD FINISHED HIS STORY, HARRY EXCUSED himself, went to the restroom, locked himself in a booth, and threw up, and for a long time he stood there taking shallow breaths and wiping his mouth and forehead with squares of toilet paper until he realized that by doing so he was turning them gold, the color of the story, or at any rate one of its colors—blood red and death-metal silver being the others—and this thought reminded him that there were several follow-up questions he would like to ask Alfonso and that there would be more than enough time later to swim out into the icy depths of his own sea of sorrows, in which, midway through Alfonso's account, he had found himself submerged, but when, after he had splashed water on the smeary makeup still covering parts of his face and straightened his hair, he got back to the table, Alfonso was gone and the booth had been occupied by a pair of teenage girls dressed like latter-day fans of the Bay City Rollers, one of whom, almost without looking up, handed him a napkin on which had been scrawled an address, a time later that evening, and the letter "A," which made Harry think of the great tale by Hawthorne, though not, or only fleetingly, of the question of adultery, but rather of the novel's deep forests filled with dense brush and gnarled trees and fallen leaves and drifts of snow and the bones of the animals and humans who had fallen there, not necessarily happily, perhaps even with their hands clasped and their heads cast heavenward, filling the empty sky with their useless piety and despair, much like, he thought with a dull shudder, his own gestures at a certain juncture, and here he still the fuck was, just like the knife-metal angel, who had once been a golden angel, whose name was Solange, who was still beautiful, even with her face broken and cast in shadow, *Solange,* he thought, whereupon two images floated like dead leaves down through his mind and landed one on top of the other, the first, of Solange, standing now farther away than ever from him on her box with the bits of metal on her face, and the other of the two of them somehow walking arm and arm along the shore, and, it seemed to him, if those thoughts could sit so close together, couldn't he, somehow, find a way to step across the inconsequential divide: perhaps, perhaps not: though, yes, really what a fool he had been to put on his paint and plastic armor and stand out in the sun and hope to be noticed by her: even if the great Don might well have done just that, he, Harry, was no great Don, he was just a sad sack from a distant country attempting, halfway around the world, some onto-logical equivalent of the Humpty Dumpty story, which of course ended in emphatic confirmation of its own disaster, in spite of the neat rhyme, "Fuck Humpty Dumpty," he said, and although he went to the trouble of extricating his duffel bag from under the table and the really quite absurdly dressed teenage girls, it was only to carry it out of the café and, with a sharp swing and hard kick, abandon it on the sidewalk outside.

THE DEAD LEAVES THAT FELL THROUGH HARRY'S HEAD IN the café were of the same species as the ones that had been falling all that day through Doña Eulalia's as she lay shivering under heavy quilts, attending to what she was convinced was a light fever but probably wasn't—she had been a life-long hypochondriac—so that when, here and there, the letter "A" began appearing among the falling bits of gold and brown and red, followed by a series of, admittedly, barely visible L's, F's, S's, N's, and O's, it took her quite some time to notice it, though when a golden horse holding a spear galloped through the downpour she sat straight up, threw off her quilts, reached for her phone and called Ireneo, who answered on the first ring, but in a hushed voice, so that she could barely hear him when he said,

"I am at my mother's bedside, Madame,"

"Ah, and how is your mother?"

"She is gravely ill, Madame,"

"I'm terribly sorry to hear it, such a shame,"

"Yes, it is distressing, Madame,"

"What do you call those horses with human heads?"

"Madame?"

"Greek mythology, devilish things,"

"Centaurs, Madame, but you must forgive me, my mother . . ."

"Yes of course, I'm so sorry, go and see the centaur on

the boulevard, the golden one, his name is Alfonso, he can tell you where to look,"

"It may be some days before I can return to the city to carry on my search, Madame,"

"Then you must go and look the moment you have returned,"

"I will, Madame, good-bye,"

"Just as soon as you have returned, make a note of it, Ireneo, and convey my best wishes to your mother, the poor woman, good-bye," said Doña Eulalia, who emitted a loud "bollocks!" as soon as she had shut her phone, and for a moment she considered asking one of the others to run the errand, but they were all—these relatives of hers—useless, not much better than the mannequins on rollers she had them drag around on the nights she had her clients over, a scheme Ireneo, the only one not related to her, had helped her come up with in order to double the number of lamps and faces—those brief, bright pools of mystery—present at her consultations, without having to reach further beyond the unpaid ranks of her family, all of whom worked for her gratis, in expectation of an inheritance . . . no, it would have to be Ireneo, and she would have to wait, she thought there was still time, "but time for what?" she asked herself as she climbed back into bed, covered herself, reached for a ther-mometer, looked for the leaves to see if anything else was galloping around in them, found that her head was empty, said, "bollocks!" again, and promptly fell asleep.

WHICH WAS JUST WHAT IRENEO, WHO HAD BEEN MORE OR
less awake since he had arrived some days previously,
wished he could do, but every time his head began to loll
his mother, who had a platoon of servants at her com-
mand but wanted only him, would moan as if on cue,
and Ireneo's hand would go out and damp her forehead
with a washcloth or squeeze a little water between her
lips, and when, in a faltering, unenthusiastic voice she
would ask him to sing, he would produce warbling,
incomplete versions of songs she had taught him during
his boyhood and made him perform, in a wig and short
pants, along with a few poorly executed dance steps, in
front of her employees at the factory during Christmas
parties, while his father, who had drunk himself to death
before Ireneo had turned ten, gazed on in poorly concealed disgust, a look which years later had found its echo
on his mother's face when he had told her he had no
interest in taking up a position in her company, and that,
instead, he had decided to go "into the occult," a field in
which if one sold one's soul at least it was on one's own
terms, and which, if less remunerative, had significant and
lasting rewards, a stance that Ireneo had continued to
maintain, even though, thus far, his role remained a supporting one, after all even now as he sat by his mother's
bed the old running shoes, which he had gone so far as
to sleep (if not bathe) in, continued to give off promising

sparks of import that he very much looked forward to being able, again, to give his full attention to, in the way, as he saw it, Doña Eulalia paid attention to the bits and pieces of information that came to her, at all hours of the day and night, which focus allowed her, most of the time, to make something like sense out of not very much at all, a skill that Harry, a few hours later, would have been very happy to have had a little of, as against his better judgment, he negotiated the gray and violet streets of the pre-dawn city on his way to Alfonso's, while at the same time continuing to think of the young woman on the plane with her book on the Black Dahlia, the man with his new golf balls, Señora Rubinski, Ireneo, Doña Eulalia with the lamp on her head, the connoisseurs, Alfonso, Solange, the young man with the knife blade in his throat, all of which had seemed to him, as he drank glass after glass of sparkling water at his kitchen table and watched the clock hands tick ever closer to this ridiculously awkward hour, like so many inexplicable blocks of ice bumping against each other on the black water that, since hearing the story of the silver angel, he had off and on been doing a dog-paddle in, any one of which he would have gladly clambered onto and taken his chances on, not least the one that corresponded to Señora Rubinski and Señora Rubinski's dead husband, whom the excellent lady had, that very evening upon his return from the café, described as they stood a moment together on the sidewalk as a most marvelous and thoughtful individual, one with whom one "always had the very best chances of passing an agreeable moment," an image that had touched Harry greatly, with the result that he had remained out on the sidewalk with Señora Rubinski for quite some time indeed, so long in fact that when Señora Rubinski announced with a sigh and a shake of her head that her husband, "a bit of a lazybones," must have fallen asleep on the couch, and that she would have to go and wake him, even though it was now far too late for them to begin their customary walk, Harry was able to offer her his arm and escort her to the elevator and, as tears began to drip down her cheeks, hand her the stray makeup-removal cloth that was still neatly folded in his front pocket, which she very elegantly used to dab at the corners of her eyes then, with a slight bow, returned to him, and as he had climbed the stairs to begin waiting to go see Alfonso, it seemed very nearly certain to him that despite the leaning of his spirits of late, Señora Rubinski's tears were about to have company, that they could not help but have company, and that this would be a good thing, for it had been a very long time, but the only tears in Harry's apartment that night were Señora Rubinski's, and of course in spite of the sparkling water that Harry found he could not stop drinking and the horrible black water it seemed to him he kept slipping below the surface of, before long the cloth that had contained them was completely dry.

HARRY COULD NOT HAVE SAID WHETHER IT WAS SOME TRICK of perception to do with the trend of his thoughts, or a pocket of unusual local phenomenon that he had stumbled into, but as he approached Alfonso's coordinates, the streets of the city, described above as gray and violet, went black then blacker, and for a moment, even though he could see quite clearly, he felt himself compelled to hold his hands pressed against his thighs, flare his nostrils, and flick his eyes back and forth as if something—possibly the air itself and how the fuck could he fight the air—was about to spring and shove a blade down his throat, or otherwise finish the job on him, what a night, what a night, but presently a cheery row of lampposts cut a series of lovely cones in the darkness and, just beyond them, he began to hear bits and pieces of birdsong, which grew stronger as he moved forward, and before very long at all he had found the address he had been looking for, pressed the intercom buzzer, and been admitted into a kind of loft by Alfonso, who, scraped clean of his gold, looked small, distinctly plump and kind, so kind that Harry, a little discombobulated and, frankly, grateful to be suddenly bathed in light, warmly pressed Alfonso's hand before accepting a large mug of coffee and a clap on the shoulder, and for a long moment he just stood there taking in the high ceiling, the crumbling paint, the wood stove in one distant corner, the black-and-white photographs of the city, interspersed with what looked like old maps of the continents and fanciful coast-lines, hanging on the walls, the piles of scrap wood here and there and the large, clean-but-paint-spattered floor, drifting, as he did so, into the kind of stupor that abrupt changes in circumstance, especially those involving shifts in temperature or quality/quantity of light rarely fail to engen-der, and it was only when Alfonso, speaking over his own mug of coffee, said, "I have something to show you," that Harry remembered what it was he had planned to say as soon as he arrived—"There are several things I'd like to ask you, Mr. Centaur,"—but instead he found himself murmur-ing, "It's very dark out," and following Alfonso to the far side of the room, and through a narrow blue door that gave onto what it took Harry a moment to realize was a garage of sorts, perhaps even—the stone seemed weathered enough—an old carriage house, in the center of which sat a large yellow submarine, more or less the one The Beatles had had their adventure in, the one that had been so use-ful in the struggle against the blue meanies, the one con-nected to the song, which he had never liked very much and which now raged very nearly out of control in his head before subsiding, slightly, then more fully, like someone had thrown a fade switch, "You can get inside it," Alfonso said,

"It's the Yellow Submarine," Harry said,

"A model, made of chicken wire and papier mâché, but a good one,"

"The song . . ." Harry said,

"It goes away, I should know, I live with the thing,"

"Did you build it?"

"I inherited it, there's a hatch, you can get inside, there's more room in it than you might think,"

"It's certainly nicely done,"

"I often climb inside it when I want a bit of quiet, after a hard day on the box, the bottom is padded, it's very nice to lie down inside it and doze,"

"I see," said Harry, taking a sip of his coffee and looking a little more carefully at Alfonso, who he suddenly understood was either drunk or medicated, but rather pleasantly so, indeed his comments about climbing into the yellow apparatus and lying down and dozing struck Harry in exactly the right way, as if he were drunk or medicated too—even though he had been neither in years—and he found himself drawing Alfonso out not on the subject of why he had invited him over at this insane hour and why, now that here he was, he was showing him this papier mâché model, but instead on the merits of lying inside the Yellow Submarine and having a snooze and feeling warm and cozy but also—that was the trick of it—vigilant, which was just as well because it turned out the answers to both sets of questions dovetailed nicely when, after a few minutes, Alfonso took his coffee mug, showed him how to open the side hatch, helped him to climb in, directed his attention to the viewing grill—hidden to the casual glance from the outside—and said, "You will be able to observe her through that, it's a camouflaging technique, often used in the military, when you've had a chance to get a feel for the inside, climb back out and we will wheel it over to the boulevard—if we get out early enough you can have the spot opposite her, it's nice isn't it, when I was young I once pitched a tent in my grandfather's attic and spent a week there, this reminds me of that,"

I've thrown away my Don Quixote costume and am in a yellow submarine, thought Harry,

"It has wheels," said Alfonso, "It's actually quite easy to push, the friend who left it here in payment of a debt pushed me around while I lay inside of it before he left, it's very comfortable to ride in, and if we were closer to the boulevard, I would offer you this pleasant experience,"

"I don't understand," said Harry,

"Why I'm doing this," said Alfonso,

"Yes," said Harry, overcoming an urge to remain on his back in the warm yellow interior and opening the hatch,

"I would be lying if I told you it was because I was the bearer of bad tidings this afternoon," said Alfonso, as the two of them began wheeling the submarine through what Harry observed with relief were the rapidly brightening streets of the city, "because I told you you weren't welcome on the boulevard in your lousy Don Quixote costume, nor because I could see, even as I had barely crested the midpoint of the story of the silver angel, which I remind you I was retelling and did not invent, that you were being deeply, troublingly affected, no, I'm doing this because as you were striking your ridiculous, amateurish poses, as you stood gushing sweat and huffing and puffing on your box, I spent no small amount of time looking at you, and while I won't go into the why of it, I thought to myself, *there's a story and a half there, a story that begins in the dark and ends in the even darker, and I would like to hear it,*"

"Everyone has a story," said Harry,

"There you trade in truisms, my friend,"

"Truisms are sort of a specialty with me,"

"I won't dispute that, it may even be true, but I would still like to hear whatever it is that has you engaging in dress-up and meeting with off-duty centaurs in the wee hours,"

"You mean besides my interest in the silver angel,"

"I mean besides your interest in the silver angel, yes,"

"And you think lending me this thing, this submarine, is going to help you get it?"

They both paused and looked at the thing in question, which rolled between them with surprising delicacy, surprising to Harry, that is, of course,

"Don't *you?*" said Alfonso,

"It's a sad story," said Harry, "so sad I don't even tell it to myself anymore,"

"So it tells itself to you," said Alfonso,

"Yes," said Harry, after a long pause, "Even though I tried to bury it, it keeps clawing its way up through the dirt—all my efforts to erase it have failed,"

"It has its way with you,"

"Something like that, and then something like . . . but that's a little silly . . ." said Harry, trailing off and wondering if, at any moment, whatever it was that was keeping him calm would be swept aside and he would howl,

"Like what?"

"I'll spare you,"

"I appreciate silly, I dress up every day like a centaur, after all," said Alfonso,

"You make a very fine centaur, I noticed you straight away," said Harry,

"Flattery is good, it is very good," said Alfonso,

"I was thinking of a syllogism, a very simple one, say, 'All people are mortal, a man's offspring were people, therefore the man's offspring were mortal,' and while, as I say, the syllogism is quite basic, more than just the middle element is missing from the conclusion, at the same time that said additional element remains not merely present, but also essential to the conclusion,"

"A haunted conclusion,"

"Yes, exactly, a haunted conclusion, the conclusion is haunted, and now I have to stop talking about it because if I don't you will see a man tear his hair out in front of your eyes,"

"Climb inside the submarine," said Alfonso, "I'll push you the rest of the way."

HARRY GOT INSIDE THE SUBMARINE WITHOUT A WORD, AND Alfonso began to push, and in the time it took them to reach the tree-lined boulevard where Alfonso left Harry, as he had promised, directly across from the silver angel's accustomed spot, the angel in question, who was still, at this early hour, just Solange, finished encasing a crumb of ginger cookie in Lucite and sat a moment staring at her work, admiring the fearful clarity of the medium, as always a little bit in love with the turgent liquidity of its hardening, the elegant curve she could still alter with fingertip, or slip her tweezers into, or some part of herself, although it would be as well, if she planned to do some Lucite diving, even just figuratively, to finish her coffee first and perhaps have another bite of her bread and rose petal jam, a jar of which Che Guevara had left outside her door in the weeks following the murder of her young man, and which had sat untouched, attracting flecks of dust and cinder, until one evening, upon returning home from a day on her box, she had scooped it up and deposited it on one of her many bare shelves, where it had continued its unopened existence until that morning, when she had looked down at her stale but salvageable bread and thought of the pale pink jam, which seemed to explode out of the jar as she opened it, then tilted the jar and let a pink glob slide down her tongue into her mouth, where after it had settled a moment it made her gasp and grab for the table to steady herself, before she tilted the jar again and gasped again, then spread some on her bread, which made her think of coffee, of how marvelous it would be to have a cup of fresh coffee to go with her bread and jam, and it wasn't until she had the coffee before her and had taken another bite, that she remembered that she had set herself the task that morning of encasing part of one of her young man's favorite cookies in Lucite, to accompany the bit of cloth from one of his purple shirts, the red plastic tine from his comb, the knob of rubber from his shoe, the button from his canvas bag, a long curled eyelash the color of burned butter, a tiny golden cog from the watch he had been in the process of taking apart, a hardened dab of bolonaise sauce from his last meal on earth, and the second word of the title, clipped from the frontispiece of his favorite book, *Paradise Lost,* and it was only when she had pulled on her latex gloves and set herself up by the open window that the sadness that for months had been circling her like a shark swept past her and looked at her with a blank, unblinking eye, but when it bit this morning, it seemed at first like it had barely broken the skin, and even when she realized that she had been mistaken, that it had indeed broken the skin and done its customary damage, she licked a drop of rose petal jam from her lips, raised one eyebrow, looked at the crumb of ginger cookie, decided it was close to finished, thought, *hmmm,* and when she got dressed for work a few minutes later, she affixed one less tear to her cheek and walked away from her building a little more quickly and with her eyes open a little more widely than usual, with the result that when she arrived at her accustomed spot—in front of a handsome old pharmacy with a medieval theme and a bustling fried fish establishment—and saw the Yellow Submarine sitting opposite her, she stood staring at it for upwards of a minute, the way, it occurred to her as she set up her box, one waking from a bad dream stares into the face of a loved one who has unexpectedly arrived at her bedside and places a calming hand on her head, and will sit there unmoving, for exactly as long as the situation warrants, which was what —though of course Solange didn't know this—Harry, looking out of the submarine through its false front grill, intended to do.

With harry in position and now far closer, in fact almost absurdly close, as we shall see, to achieving his goal, the silver angel feeling ever-so-slightly better and already looking over, with interest, in Harry's direction, Alfonso climbing onto his own box and leaning into his hind legs to begin the long day, a warm breeze beginning to blow up from the sea, tourists streaming in and out of the market, shop doors opening and closing and old men and women taking up their stations in shadowy doorways and windows, it is time for the connoisseurs to take their morning walk, an undertaking they execute with a measure of determined intimacy: shoulder to shoulder, though not arm in arm, matching watery gray eyes flicking this way and that like small birds in their cages leaping from bar to bar, which is to say they take it all in, these connoisseurs, and not just the shining breeze-blessed surfaces, which drive the eyes of the tourists mad with desire, but also the peripheral zones, where bits of old candy conspire with crushed soda cans and melting cubes of ice to haunt the secondary and tertiary corners of the mind, zones that the connoisseurs, who have been taking daily walks up and down the boulevard for much longer than Alfonso and his colleagues suspect, long ago learned to attend to and make use of: the corners of the mind and what makes its way into them being dynamic crossroads full of wounding vapors and fierce reflections and, as one of them once put it to the other during their endless walkings up and walkings down the boulevard and surrounding streets to check on their charges, certainly, but also, as we shall see later, to accomplish other, darker tasks, but on this morning they merely walk and observe and, occasionally, talk, as they do briefly to the silver angel—"She looks gorgeous today, don't you think? She's not crying as much as yesterday"—and, even more briefly, to the inhabitant of the Yellow Submarine—"Much fucking better, friend,"—and in between times they whistle atonal airs that infect the thought processes of more than one person they pass, including, on the edge of the small crowd gathered to watch the living trees sway, as they do twice each fifteen minutes on calm days and even more frequently on breezy ones like today, a young woman with hair the color of crushed pomegranate, who will spend the rest of the day, without knowing why, humming a tune that she's never heard before and that, outside of dream, she will never hear again, not least because her time in the city and its environs has come almost to its end, and after weeks of popping in and out of museums, where more often than she cared for her thoughts turned to the surrealists and the Black Dahlia killing, with the effect that in the contemporary art museum, as she stood in front of Man Ray's portrait of Miró, she began to believe that the gray-faced man standing next to her in an orange trench coat and blue ball cap was a murderer, and then, a moment later, that she was in the museum gathering inspiration for her own next killing, which she would accomplish by means of injecting fuchsia dye into the veins of the first old granny she could get her hands on and hogtie in an empty courtyard as the clock struck thirteen and the walls began to sprout cornflowers, etc.: it has been a strange time in the city for the young woman, whose jet-black roots, it must be said, are starting to show, a detail that Harry in his Yellow Submarine can't help noticing, because the young woman, after giving the submarine a casual glance, bends over in front of the concealed grill to tie her shoe, and lets her hair cascade down over her face, causing Harry, looking away while she pauses in front of his hiding place, to smile in recognition, and to almost blurt out, "Hi, it's me from the plane," but after opening himself up, if one can put it that way, to Alfonso as they made their way to the boulevard, his self-censor put a firm hand on his shoulder and said, "don't say a word, don't even breathe, don't let anyone else know you're here," and by the time he says, "fuck you," to his self–censor, which feels good, the young woman has turned on her heel and walked off as if she has just remembered something, which she has: a butcher shop she hopes to reach before they have sold out of a particular cut of beef she is fond of, and while soon she will have left these pages forever, her unexpected appearance before the Yellow Submarine, coming so soon after that of the connoisseurs, sets up an important association in Harry's mind, which goes through several stages of transformation in the coming hours, involving on the one hand the Black Dahlia, golf balls, fuselages, his own sorry story, knife blades, and the silver angel—who Harry is sure keeps looking over at him, or rather at his submarine—and on the other, the three old guys who pass him twice more before they vanish off to wherever it is they go to refuel, so that, eventually, as Harry lies there looking out at the world, which has been so pleasantly reduced to a tissue-covered oval grate, the phrase "death and the connoisseurs" plays over and over again in his head, though with different intonations, and after a while the repetitions start to feel almost like he is struggling to remember something that has gotten stuck and is simultaneously thumbing its nose at him and teetering on the tip of his tongue, while the repetitions occurring in the head of the young woman with hair the color of crushed pomegranates, of the atonal air effectively implanted there by the three old men, which she considers later, as she polishes off her favored cut of beef and the remains of a few string beans sautéed in salted butter, and begins to think of getting her suitcases in order, make her remember a brightly lit swimming pool she once plunged painfully into over and over again one summer night long ago, as she attempted with no success to teach herself how to perform a backflip.

II

*The past, since it does not exist, is
hard to erase. Tears and the gnashing
of teeth.*

THIS MOVE, THE DIFFICULT, PERHAPS IMPOSSIBLE PERFOR-
mance of which many of us can commiserate with, in
which the body leaps up and back, while time, of course,
continues to move forward, might be diverting enough to
stop a moment and consider—picture for example the long
gorgeous lift of the Olympic athlete in the midst of a perfect floor exercise, or the delicate, deadly grace of the
Shaolin Temple Kung Fu master flipping backwards,
through a snow shower, above waving bamboo, or a
determined teenaged girl crashing backwards over and
over again into bright blue water—as having teetered for a
moment at the midpoint of this story, the days again
began to slip by, and while it might be interesting to consider in greater detail, for example, how Ireneo came to the
conclusion that his mother was, if not faking her illness,
then certainly exaggerating its extent, and that in conse-
quence his presence at her bedside was no longer required,
and that he might just as well slip out in the middle of the
night and run most of the way back to the city, where,
after paying a brief visit to Doña Eulalia, who had recov-
ered from her own dubious illness and informed him that,
as she sensed the situation regarding the first individual
with the broken face had been greatly ameliorated and that
communicating with her was now merely a matter of pro-
fessional courtesy, finding Harry, for whom the situation
was worsening, should be his priority, he made haste for

the boulevard and an interview with the centaur, who, at the end of his shift, told him that the individual he was searching for could be found in such and such a part of the city, or how it was that one balmy evening, and not for the first time, Solange—whose curiosity and progressive warming had led her to remove her silver tears one by one and take concomitant, exploratory steps across the boulevard in the direction of the improbable, appealing yellow apparition—came to be leaning, with a slight smile gracing her never-smiling silver lips, against the side of the Yellow Submarine, while Harry, heart smashing up and down inside him, lay just a papier mâché wall away from her, whistling a sort of Beatles medley, we could just say that while time has moved forward, some not insignificant back-flipping has occurred, and consequently, we are no longer quite where we last were, a statement that, if we accept the notion that complexity is derived from the intricate and unexpected arrangement of banalities, we can be content with, though perhaps not in the stomach-fluttering way that Harry was content to be lying where he was lying, more like in the understatedly pleased way that Ireneo was content to be running in the city again, even following a piste he was absolutely certain was an incorrect one, that Harry wouldn't be anywhere near the arcaded renaissance courtyard the tricky-looking centaur had directed him to, that all he would find there would be the usual motley assortment of northern European group-tour participants, some wearing ball caps and/or T-shirts proclaiming their affiliations, as with unadulterated pleasure—convinced they were at last, after a series of false starts, in the midst of an authentic moment—they gobbled second-rate tidbits thawed and deep fried in filthy kitchens hiding behind ornate exteriors, which is exactly what Ireneo did find and had plenty of time to consider, and from multiple angles, as for good measure he ran several slow laps waiting to see if Harry would make an appearance on the terrace of the grand café under the arches, where Bavarians ate fried potatoes and bruschetta with such infectious gusto that eventually Ireneo plopped down at an empty table and ordered a large bottle of sparkling water and a plateful of potatoes, while his running shoes, no worse for wear after his long run down the coast, and certainly no more silent, burbled on, as they had been doing all morning, about trust, about placing one's fate in the hands of strangers, about clandestine meetings under facades carved from stone in the desert and trysts carried out in rooms lit by low-grade electricity derived from enormous water wheels, a theme that had switched around by the time Ireneo began attacking his fried potatoes—which he dipped in crab mayonnaise—in earnest, to a discussion first of modes of conveyance in general and then of underwater modes of conveyance in particular, and as Ireneo lifted his glass of water and held it aloft so that the backlit tables full of Bavarians looked like the bits of shifting color in a kaleidoscope, he said, "Ah, for fuck's sake," put his glass down, ate his last fried potato, and ran back to the boulevard, though by the time he had reached it night had fallen and all the statues and the submarine had gone.

IT MIGHT BE TOO MUCH TO REQUEST OF THE READER, ALREADY asked for a good deal of indulgence in the matter of the backflips, to imagine that while Ireneo was running his laps, eating his potatoes, and listening to his shoes, Harry stopped whistling, swallowed deeply, and started speaking, and that, after stressing that he was an acquaintance of the submarine's owner, Alfonso, who of course was well known to Solange (a fact she confirmed), part of what Harry eventually said was, "There's plenty of room, would you like to see what this is like on the inside," and that Solange surprised no one more than herself by saying, "Yes," and that, further, Alfonso, who each evening helped Harry return the submarine to its garage, appeared at a propitious moment, understood immediately, even though the interior of the submarine was dead silent, what had transpired and asked the two of them if they might be interested in a ride, the response to which was a muffled "All right," from one voice, or the other, or both, Alfonso thought, as he disengaged the submarine and, with only slightly more trouble than he had had in pushing Harry by himself, rolled them first down the boulevard—the remnants of the day's crowds parting before them with smiles and cameras cocked—and then along one gently curving street and quiet plaza after another, with here and there a splashing fountain, which transformed the sticky pavement beneath his feet, illuminated by shop windows and the occasional streetlamp, into the surface of an unnamed body of water, and that it crossed Harry's mind, as he lay now just inches from Solange's silver face, neither of them saying a word, their silence seeming like the first part of an understanding, that Alfonso was a kind of gondolier and the submarine a gondola and the streets watery thoroughfares, while Solange thought, *we are in a submarine, protected from the terrible depths, and the lights we can see through the grill are the entrances to grottos,* although of course they both thought many other things, especially when Alfonso paused for a moment before a pair of skeleton puppets, one playing a grand piano, the other a violin, the music being emitted from a gramophone standing between the two young women discretely working the marvelous puppets not anything either of them could have named, though we might as well note that it was Brahms, a jaunty piece that, being played as it was by the two little skeletons in their evening wear, seemed to color the air in the submarine an opalescent indigo that sent them both swimming off together into the depths Solange had imagined and Harry had intuited, and that, finally, Alfonso rolled the Yellow Submarine up to the gaily lit window of one of the grottos that both of them had looked upon with greatest interest and asked the two submariners if they might be interested in debarking, momentarily, in order to attend a small, convivial gathering of friends, with the understanding that he, Alfonso, would be prepared to set out again at a moment's notice should a hasty departure seem indicated . . . but this is more or less what occurred, and Harry and Solange, who had begun their day on opposite sides of the boulevard, found themselves near the end of it in the company of Alfonso, enveloped in a cloud of growing familiarity that felt as freshly promising to both of them as a shower of melting snow falling against a backdrop of pure blue sky, stepping together through the doorway of a gallery opposite the city's great cathedral—the very one where Ireneo, now on his way home to await Harry's reappearance on the boulevard the following day, most frequently lit his candles—and into a small crowd of off-duty living statues that burst into spontaneous applause when they saw Solange, whom they hadn't seen off the boulevard in ages, and for several minutes she was swept away into a collective embrace that gave Harry the opportunity to turn to Alfonso and thank him, and for Alfonso to bow and say, "You still owe me your story, and not just its outline,"

"It may have a new ending,"

"We can only hope,"

"Yes, yes we certainly can."

DRINKS AT THE EVENT THEY WERE ATTENDING WERE PRO-cured by pushing one of two buttons set close together near the baseboard beneath the front window, which prompted a slender hand to appear out of a small hole cut into the floor, a hand that would, when given a modest amount of money, reemerge with an ice-cold bottle of sparkling water, or a glass of grenadine, or a chocolate malt, while donations to the gallery hosting the event could be made by holding a bill under a piece of nearby plastic tubing that snaked its way up to the ceiling where it curved around and around before plunging into a clear receptacle, already well supplied with bills that would dance madly when a button near the opening on the other side of the room was pushed and a fresh bill was sucked into it, a seductive spectacle that deprived both Harry, holding a chocolate malt, and Solange, a glass of grenadine, of several bills each, and if a line had not begun to form behind them they might well have allowed the contraption to suck up the entire collective contents of their wallets, which would have been a shame because, as they discovered, feeding additional bills into a slot in the floor caused a room that housed a griffon's skeleton to light up under the oak plank-ing, and furthermore there were tempting deep-fried items on offer at back tables that Alfonso convinced them to sam-ple, and so it was that Harry drank a chocolate malt and ate a deep-fried clove cookie while silver-faced Solange interspersed bites of deep-fried almond butter squares with sips of grenadine and waves at Julius Caesar, Atlas, and Che Guevara, the latter who ran straight over, stuffed his unlit cigar in his mouth, and gave Solange a bear hug, lifting her straight off the floor and twirling her around, before turning to Harry, bowing, and suggesting that the two of them take the air, that it was a splendid night, there was a marvelous little garden attached to the store, etc.,

"Well," Harry said,

"Go on, go on, Raimon is an old friend," Solange said,

"And that's really why I wanted to have a word," said Raimon, once they had made their way through a back room and into what was indeed a thoroughly charming tree-filled garden, lit with strings of lights that were reflected in a handsome, merrily plashing pond surrounded by high walls, one of which, according to Raimon, who lit a red cigar and leaned against an ornamental quince, had been built by the Romans as part of the ancient city's outer defenses, many relics of which Harry couldn't have failed to notice were still standing amidst the modern edifices,

"Fascinating," said Harry,

"Yes," said Raimon, "Though of course every now and again some section of wall, uncared for by the municipal authorities, crumbles to the ground, leaving only its absence behind,"

"Its absence . . ."

"Its afterglow, in which some aspect of the former wall might be said to remain standing,"

"I like that," Harry said,

"Are you familiar with negativity delirium?" Raimon asked,

"No," Harry said,

"It's the evil inverse of phantom limb syndrome, whereby, rather than missing limbs and organs maintaining their presence, present limbs and organs vanish,"

"That's awful,"

"It's diabolical,"

"I've often thought of chopping off my legs, because of the condition I suffer from, but now I can see that they might not be so easy to get rid of,"

"Not so easy at all, take for example, the case of my missing hands," said Raimon, wedging his brightly burning cigar in the corner of his mouth and holding his hands up in the air,

"What are those things?" said Harry,

"You can see them too?"

"Your hands, yes,"

"Not everyone can see them,"

"How extraordinary,"

"It's the greatest mystery and speaks to the core of this whole business, which is to say that they've come back, but not quite the same and not quite in the right place,"

"Yikes," said Harry,

"I've never heard of such a case and I've done a great amount of research," said Raimon,

"Nor have I," said Harry, for lack of anything terribly apropos to offer, while trying and failing to see in what way the hands were wrongly placed,

"If it were an instance of phantom limb syndrome, we might not be surprised to know that the limb in question had returned, in fact it is quite common for them to return to the wrong place, my own uncle lost his left ring finger to a ripsaw and had it return some months later in between the middle and index finger of his right hand—it was most distressing for him and all of us, but this is an instance of negativity delirium in which what has vanished returns and is visible, at least to some,"

Harry wasn't quite sure what to say to this either so contented himself to raise an eyebrow and nod in an enabling manner,

"Shall we go back inside?" Raimon said, looking at his hands and shrugging, as if there was nothing further that could or should be said,

"Yes," said Harry,

"I'm glad we had a chance to chat,"

"I am too,"

"That's really all I wanted, was to chat,"

"I'm glad we could,"

"She's had a very rough time of it,"

"So I gather,"

"You could say that the universe has conspired against her,"

"I'm in a position to empathize,"

"I'm so very sorry,"

"Thank you,"

"It is all much more difficult than it ought to be, isn't it?"

"It is indeed," Harry said.

THE STATUES PRESENT WERE EITHER IN PARTIAL OR COMPLETE costume, which gave the wonder-filled room, through the front window of which the Yellow Submarine was fully visible, the air of a carnival, or, when Cleopatra and the Willow Tree began dancing next to the deep-fryers, of a masked ball, so that for a time after his return from the garden, and his only very slightly unnerving conversation with Raimon, whom he had rather liked, Harry's happiness knew, as they say, no bounds, and when the Oak Tree pulled him up off his feet to dance next to the deep-fryers he did not decline, and for a few minutes he shimmied and whirled with a gusto that probably, at his age, did him no credit, but he would have continued and perhaps even pulled Solange up off her feet had he not, in looking over at her, realized that she was sagging, that the moment, such as it had been, was passing, and that it was time to get back in the submarine and sail off into the night, a course of action that, upon his suggestion, appealed to her, and that was agreeable to Alfonso, and so after finishing their food and saying good-bye, Harry and Solange climbed back into the submarine, though not before catching sight of the connoisseurs, who were just that moment arriving at the gallery, and while they were already in the submarine and rolling when the connoisseurs passed them and bade them each, by name, good-night, Harry felt Solange shiver for a moment beside him, and, although he knew it was indiscreet, could not refrain from asking her what it was,

"Nothing, fatigue," she said,

"I understand," Harry said, registering, as he did so, that by responding in this way, he had completed a problematic circuit, across the poles of which a bright blue band of falsehood was now crackling—she had not shivered, he was sure, because of a chill, and he had not, strictly speaking, understood anything, even if the unwelcome phrase "death and the connoisseurs" appeared for a moment before vanishing—but Harry also registered that every incipient relationship is at least partially lit by the light of dubious complicity so he simply smiled in the blue light and they continued on their way in silence, Harry thankfully not thinking about the connoisseurs, but about negativity delirium, which just about summed it all up, then about different qualities and kinds of illumination, and the structures that best masked or presented them, and Solange about the cold efficiency with which the connoisseurs had told and retold her story— which she suspected Harry had heard, probably from Alfonso, a story addict if ever there was one, because of the gentle way he, Harry, had remarked earlier, before she had actually laid eyes on him, that the last of her tears was gone—but also about the way Harry had probed for a moment, but not pushed, had allowed her her lie of convenience without forcing her to enlarge it, or to ask him to leave well enough alone, the sort of direct statement that, uttered too early, can have unfortunate results, often because of misinterpretation, which, the thought occurred to her, had too often marred her interactions with her young man who, likely because of his youth, which if not extreme had nevertheless been considerable, had gotten it wrong, so to speak, with some frequency, which in the short term had seemed endearing, but over the long term . . . well there hadn't been any long term, and whereof, she thought, we cannot speak, thereof we ought to keep our mental mouths shut and reach for the Lucite, or rose petal jam, another jar of which she had purchased that morning and had told Raimon about that night, just after he had told her that if what he thought was occurring with Harry was actually occurring then he approved: she licked her lips, which still had a few flecks of almond butter on them and thought,

But why don't I feel more sad?

It's this submarine, plain and simple, thought Harry, whose mind had been moving along a roughly parallel track, as it had been, or as it seemed to Harry to have been, with the man under the awning,

It's like spending time in a hollowed-out Twinkie, thought Solange, who as a foreign exchange student in Lawrence, Kansas had eaten plenty of them,

The thing even smells good, thought Harry,

"What a beautiful night," they both said,

and the coincidence, though startling after so long a silence, didn't seem as extraordinary as it might have given that what they could suddenly see out of the front grill, the half-lit trunks of palms along the beach and ship lights sparkling here and there across the moonlit bay, was indeed beautiful,

"This is a fine spot, I'm going to leave you here," Alfonso said,

"We can roll it back together," Solange said, and though both of them were sorry to see Alfonso, who came around and put his smiling, still-golden face in the grill, go, it seemed somehow appropriate that they would now have some time even more alone, even if as it turned out it was just to lie there very close to each other and look out over the glittering bay before debarking and making their slow way home through a night that seemed to rise and fall, enormous, like the sea they had left behind them—the sea, as Solange had called it, of commas, each wave a phrase in a sentence that was never quite finished, that would never quite be finished, until of a dreadful sudden it was—to bask separately in the mystery of what was occurring, this gently promising something that felt like it was happening to them.

As harry and solange were drifting off into a short sleep, Ireneo, who had spent more than half the night running down the city's glowing avenues, rose and took off his shoes, then showered and put his shoes back on and went to see Doña Eulalia, who had asked him, when he had phoned her the previous evening to report, to come and see her at sunrise, a request that she had promptly forgotten, with the result that when Ireneo let himself in and knocked on her bedroom door, she was still, and not for the last time during this account, deep asleep, and was not pleased to be woken, and called Ireneo "Imbecile," which he did not like, nor, apparently, did his shoes, for they barked out a retaliatory "Smelly old bag" and one or two other epithets that Ireneo, operating under the impression that the shoes spoke to him and him alone, was inclined to thank them for, except that as soon as the epithets had been uttered Doña Eulalia switched on the bedside light, reached for her glasses, peered down at the shoes, then up at Ireneo, at whom she smiled and said, "I once had a pair like that, they are great fun and even useful until they lead you astray, I threw mine into a furnace after they suggested I cut off my index finger and feed it to the cat, but not before, mind you, getting out a kitchen knife and sharpening it, thank God my late husband, who had never liked the look of them, came in and made me take them off, what have yours been saying besides 'smelly old bag'?"

"After the centaur sent me off on a goose chase they told me where to look,"

"For which bit of information I'm inclined to forgive them their insults, though I'm not as inclined, my boy, to forgive you for finding them so agreeably apropos,"

"You *had* just called me 'imbecile,' Madame,"

"And so of course I had, for which I apologize, but at any rate, time is almost up and I must see Harry tonight, no more delays,"

"I'll speak to him first thing this morning,"

"Good, and Ireneo,"

"Yes, Madame,"

"Do I smell?"

"You do not, Madame,"

"I'm relieved, you will watch out for those shoes, they will have you running out in front of cars before long,"

"I will,"

"Then that's excellent, I'll expect you tonight,"

"Good-bye, Madame," Ireneo said and left the house and immediately started running, but when his shoes began to speak—small recriminations and half-hearted defenses—Ireneo stopped and said, "I'm on to you," whereupon the shoes fell silent, and Ireneo headed off at a trot to a stand in the market, which opened early and served passable coffee and stuffed pastries, over which, while the curiously invigorating smell of the arriving fish, fruit, and freshly butchered meat wafted past, he could linger until it was time to go and see Harry and put an end to this errand, which had, after all, gone on much longer than should have been necessary, sentiments that overlapped in substantive ways with those being experienced, at that very moment at another market stand that served passable coffee but exceptional pastries, by Alfonso, who was perched, somewhat less comfortably than he cared to be between the connoisseurs, who were much less the worse for wear than he was for having spent the night eating deep fried foods and slurping down chocolate malts at the gallery, where Alfonso had returned after leaving Harry and Solange, not because he had wished to round out his evening with further celebratory activity, but because, at the precise moment that Solange shivered in the Yellow Submarine, one of the connoisseurs had slipped him a note that read, "Come back and see us when you are finished," and for Alfonso, who had been a grateful recipient of the con- noisseurs' largesse for longer than any other current statue on the boulevard, a request from them was as good as a com- mand, but that they were interested in anything more than his presence on the dance floor as the party trundled on into the wee hours was left unclear until, not terribly long before day- break, they had danced a moment on either side of and in front of him then taken him by the arms and led him in the direction, as they put it, of a place they could all chat—this stand in the market where the connoisseurs were habitués— about, as it occurred, Harry and, by extension, Solange,

"So, it's working," one of them said,

"And part of why we asked you to join us for break- fast is just to express the sentiment . . ."

"The conviction,"

"Yeah, the conviction that it couldn't have been done without your help,"

"My help?" said Alfonso, the connoisseurs laughed, one of them gave out a short whistle, then another one clapped him on the shoulder and said,

"No need to be disingenuous,"

"It's unappealing,"

"Unappetizing,"

"It's like all that fried food at the party,"

"Gets to you,"

"Only with this you don't want to keep eating,"

"You don't want to start eating," the connoisseurs each picked up the cream-filled pastry they had ordered, wrinkled their noses, and tossed it back onto the counter, while Alfonso, who had a large bite of a similar pastry in his mouth, swallowed slowly, thought of telling Harry the story, of giving him the use of the submarine and putting him into position opposite Solange, of helping him push it each morning, of offering to roll him and Solange through the warm streets, and tried to decide if he had known he was helping, that he was acting, in a sense, as an instrument, but found he couldn't quite remember, not that it mattered so much, he was happy to help and said as much and the connoisseurs picked up their pastries again and took bites and one of them said,

"Sending that guy off last night was the best thing you did,"

"Stroke of genius,"

"Maybe not genius but it bought us some time,"

"Come on, this is Alfonso, our friend, let's call it genius, we can call it genius,"

"For fuck's sake, fine, it was a stroke of genius,"

"Gave Harry his night,"

"And what a night,"

"All it takes is one,"

"For love to come knocking,"

"Now it doesn't matter,"

"They're both hooked,"

"Hooked enough, Solange'll get over it,"

"Teach her a little lesson, she'll be fine,"

"Why would Solange, of all people, need to be taught a lesson?" Alfonso asked, prompting two of the connoisseurs to smack the other and say,

"He misspoke, he was thinking about something else,"

"Criminy, you're right, I misspoke, I *was* thinking about something else, apologies, Jesus, of course, poor Solange,"

"This is about him,"

"Harry,"

"Don Quixote,"

"Ha, ha, ha,"

"Now it can start,"

"What can?" said Alfonso,

"Ah, the poor schmuck," said one of the connoisseurs,

"Yeah, the poor schmuck," the other said.

THE POOR SCHMUCK WAS FEELING LIKE ANYTHING BUT AS HE stood in front of the mirror in his apartment—first smoothing down the slightly wrinkled jeans he had left too long in the pile of clean laundry without folding, then smoothing the short sleeves of his yellow T-shirt with its blue sea bass logo, then pulling on his brown jacket, which did surprisingly well in warm weather, then running his hands through his still-wet hair, which, he had a feeling, would fall wrong all day, despite the solid quantity of hair paste he had applied after washing it—in fact he was feeling almost what one could call excellent, even better than he had felt when he had still been feeling good on the evening he had first met Ireneo and seen Solange, and the prospect of the day about to unfurl before him was so appealing that once or twice as he was going about his ablutions and eating his sausage and bread covered in the extraordinary rose petal jam that Solange had insisted on running inside to get for him when he had dropped her off at her apartment just a few hours previously, he had burst into song, the submarine thing, yes, but also bits and pieces of others that he had not come up with in years, and indeed he was in the explosive middle of one of these bits when he stepped through the doors of his building a few minutes after leaving his mirror behind and ran into Señora Rubinski, who, beaming, said, "Ah, Harry, how perfect, perhaps you would like to join us, my

sleepyhead is finally up off the couch, we're off for a morning walk, no need to wait for evening, here he is," upon
which she indicated, with rather a flourish, an elderly gentleman, the spitting image of the picture Señora Rubinski
carried with her, who smiled a little sheepishly, shrugged,
and seemed not at all nonplussed by Harry's rather stunned
silence at being presented to a man he could see through,
even if only a little—at the right shoulder and the left shin—
nor did Señora Rubinski, who had a reputation for moder-
ate prickliness, take poorly Harry's silence, which went on
for the entire time the three of them were standing there,
although when after an awkward interval Harry's hand
went slowly up and out, as if in spite of Harry's reluctance
it had decided a proper greeting was in order, a tiny cloud
of worry came and rained on the edges of her huge smile,
and she bade Harry a hasty farewell and, not quite touch-
ing the small of Señor Rubinski's back, ushered him away,
leaving Harry standing there staring after them, at Señor
Rubinski in particular, though not, as one might imagine,
with his hand still theatrically stretched out before him—he
had immediately pulled that back in, placed it in his pocket,
and made a nice tight fist of it—thinking, O.K. . . . and then,
probably because he had thought it the night before as he
and Solange had stood up straight after climbing out of the
submarine and saw both Venus and the moon reflected on
the disturbingly shiny waters of the bay, which looked
both like and unlike the endless, gentle waters they had
seemed to swim through together earlier, *It harrows me with
fear and wonder,* the overly poetic incongruity of which
remark, not to mention the terrors to do with numbness
and icy water it adumbrated, had kept him from voicing it

then but didn't stop him from murmuring it now as the Rubinskis turned a corner and vanished, and he began making his way to Alfonso's to collect the submarine and head for the boulevard, with the result that Harry arrived at his now customary spot in a very different frame of mind indeed and the silence that surrounded him inside the submarine, which found itself amplified by Solange's absence from her box across the boulevard, even though it was past the hour they had spoken of the night before, was for the first time an uncomfortable, almost an untenable silence, a silence harrowed, in short, by fear and wonder, in that uncomfortable order, and so when Ireneo jogged up to the grill of the submarine and cleared his throat, Harry threw open the hatch and stepped out and, without hesitation, vigorously pumped the very real Ireneo's proffered hand, an operation that was only mildly complicated by Ireneo's apparent reluctance to stop jogging in place as he delivered his message.

"S<small>HE WANTS TO SEE</small> *ME*?" <small>HARRY SAID</small>,

"Yes," Ireneo said,

"You're sure you've got the right person?"

"More than,"

"Because if it's Solange you're looking for she'll be here any minute,"

"Solange . . ."

"The silver angel, the one with the broken face, the one you were looking for,"

"The two of you have struck up an acquaintance,"

"We have, after that night I looked for both of you and found her,"

"Well, my employer would be very happy to greet Solange too, but it's really you, Harry, she is now eager to speak with,"

"Why?"

"I don't know,"

"I met a ghost this morning,"

"A ghost?"

"My neighbor's dead husband, an older gentleman, he has been dead for years,"

"But now he's not,"

"Well, I suppose technically, of course, he still is,"

"I see, yes, not so terribly odd in and of itself, but I'll let my employer know, it might be related,"

"To what?"

"I don't know, in fact, I have no idea," having said this, Ireneo swept a long finger across his forehead, simultaneously removing a fat bead of sweat that had been threatening to fall at any moment and adjusting the placement of an errant lock of damp black hair,

"Look, if you don't mind my asking," said Harry, "Why are you running in place?"

"That's a long story too, but I can stop any time I want, in case you are wondering,"

"No, I wasn't wondering that,"

"Well, I can, but that's not important, what is important is that you accompany me tonight,"

"I'd be delighted to,"

"Excellent, I'll come and collect you here,"

"What if we meet at the café again, that will give me a chance to get the submarine back where it belongs,"

"I'll look for you there, just after sunset,"

"Fine," Harry said, then watched as Ireneo not only jogged off at a brisk pace, but looked down at his feet as he did so and said, "Shut up," only to come to a dead halt a few paces later, pull off his shoes, throw them against the side of a flower kiosk, start off down the boulevard, barefoot this time, then reappear a moment later, somewhat sheepishly grab up the shoes, and wave at Harry—who felt a little bad for having played witness to such a perplexing sequence of events, and pretended to be looking elsewhere—then put them on and ran off again, clearly muttering to himself, giving, in other words, every indication that he was undergoing some sort of psychotic episode, and while it wouldn't be accurate to say that Harry's attitude at watching Ireneo charge noisily off was identical to the one that had struck him earlier in the presence of the Rubinskis, the overlap was enough to make him wince a little at the thought of returning to the state he had been in before Ireneo had appeared and, a moment later, actually clap his hands and give a little jump when he realized that Solange was standing on the other side of the boulevard smiling at him.

IT TOOK SOLANGE A MOMENT TO REGISTER THAT THE INTER-
twining of pleasure and concern that she felt dancing
across her face as she watched Harry was *actually* dancing
across her face, in a kind of variable speed tango, rather
than remaining just below its painted surface, and then a
moment longer to remember that as she had sat in her
apartment applying her silver makeup earlier she had been
overcome with an urge to twist and contort her face, to
make it do, as she had said to herself, things it hadn't done
in a long time, which hadn't meant very much to her then
as she had made faces at herself in the mirror, but seemed
to have more than a little resonance now, as Harry came
quickly across the boulevard toward her and the tango
stopped as concern bowed and stepped aside, abandoning
the floor to pleasure, which did a pirouette and splits, and
she felt her face breaking into an outrageous grin, the kind
she had once been capable of achieving at a moment's
notice but that had vanished with her young man and gold
face paint, and Harry, looking at the grin that had come out
to greet him thought, if I ran fast enough and dove I could
end up inside that smile and wouldn't we both be surprised, but Harry didn't speed up and dive, in fact he
slowed down a little as he approached and the smile that
lit his face grew softer as he approached, and for a fraction
of a second Solange thought, without quite knowing why,
We're both climbing, but in opposite directions, and then Harry

was standing before her, his eyes beaming, his graying hair catching the light surrounding them, and she was telling him about sitting in front of the mirror that morning making faces and that suddenly now, even though she hadn't slept at all and was in desperate need of a cup of coffee and a bucket full of pastries, she couldn't stop grinning and felt like a second-string circus clown, and Harry was saying, let's go get coffee and a couple hundred pastries, which is more or less what they did—at a third stand at the edge of the market, one Solange had long frequented and which gave them a view both of the Yellow Submarine and the pile of Solange's gear, which she had left in a heap on her box—and to say that both of them were delighted that the awkwardness they had been aware might be present when they met again in broad daylight did not materialize, would be an understatement of the first order, to borrow the phrase that ran through Harry's mind as they sat there on their stools at a stand that marked the third point in a roughly isosceles triangle formed by the market's three coffee stands, the two longer, equidistant lines of which converged on Harry and Solange and their plates full of pastries, which is pretty to think of but also satisfying to note given that, Ireneo having already impacted on Harry's day, the connoisseurs and Alfonso slid off their own stools and a moment later passed within view of Solange, who had just enough trouble interpreting what struck her as a curiously painful disjunction between the placid faces of the connoisseurs on the one hand and the markedly unplacid face of Alfonso on the other, that she elbowed Harry, pointed at the foursome, which had stopped a moment at the edge of the market to wait for a dolly piled high with battered fish carcasses to trundle by, and quietly asked if she thought they looked "odd" to him, and Harry said they certainly did,

"They make me shiver, those three, as I'm sure you noticed last night, even if you were too discreet to discuss it," said Solange, her frame vibrating with such force this time that Harry immediately rejected his first impulse, which was to tell her that the three of them made him think of death, then failed to abstain from placing his hand on hers for a moment, a move that filled him with just enough trepidation to make him take it away almost as soon as he had touched her, but Solange, who had been gazing off into space for a moment, with her grin, which had naturally been subsiding anyway, now completely collapsed, came back from wherever—for she couldn't have quite said herself—her shivering had taken her, looked Harry in the eye and said,

"Put that paw back over here," and after he had covered her hand again and they had sat there a few minutes without speaking in the center of a cliché that would have struck them both as smashing had they discussed it, Solange said,

"We barely know each other, Harry,"

and Harry said, "That's true,"

and Solange said, "Let's address that."

As SOLANGE AND HARRY DEEPENED THEIR ACQUAINTANCE—AT the coffee stand, against the Yellow Submarine, along the boulevard and the beach and then on Harry's bed— Alfonso excused himself from the connoisseurs, donned his regalia, leaned back into his hind legs and became a golden centaur, and although he was every bit as magnificent and clearly impressive to the heavy crowds on that day as he was on all the others, behind the gold paint and the shining plastic armor he was filled with more misgiving than his sanguine outlook would generally have indicated, not because, he thought, the connoisseurs had asked him to implicate himself any further in whatever scheme it was they were cooking up, besides relieving Harry of his Yellow-Submarine privileges, which in any case—they had said and he had concurred—Harry didn't need anymore now that he had "gotten the girl," but rather because he was no longer sure if it would be fair, in the context of the deception he, Alfonso, was clearly helping to perpetrate, to press Harry to tell him his story, which he really did very much want to hear and which, he knew, and here was the source, or so he thought, of his misgiving, he *would absolutely* press him to tell, regardless of this question of fairness, and the truth was it remained to be seen whether or not what he had done for Harry—rather, obviously, than *to* Harry—which had paved the way for an interview with Solange, and, he thought, probably much more, would retrospectively be seen as a favor: there was some bad business in store for the "poor schmuck"—the connoisseurs never exaggerated and they never lied—but just how bad wasn't clear . . . , and now that we've had a taste of Alfonso's not-altogether-admirable line of thought, which continued untainted by any genuine feeling of remorse for most of the afternoon, though not, as we will see, throughout the evening, it might be as well, while we allow Harry and Solange another few hours to exchange stories and hint at others, to tell each other about the ghosts of dead husbands and knife blades and broken faces and black dahlias and shivering fits, but also about other things, a nearby cliff covered in flowers, a favorite novel, the surprising pleasures of working with Lucite, a beach that glowed pale violet in the moonlight, to attend a bit to Ireneo, who as you will recall we left in the midst of an apparent argument with his disgruntled running shoes, which even before Ireneo had left his stand in the market to come and speak to Harry, had set aside their silence and launched into a tirade against both Doña Eulalia and Ireneo himself to do with their stunning incompetence and the shoes' manifest perspicacity, a tirade that only grew in volume during Ireneo's conversation with Harry next to the Yellow Submarine and that culminated in a string of epithets so palpably vile that Ireneo tore the shoes off and threw them against the flower stand only to, a moment later, pick them up again and put them back on his feet, whereupon they started cooing and pointing out that not all sinister pairs of shoes were alike no matter what Doña Eulalia had said, and that there were many other factoids that they could share with Ireneo, should he care to keep running and continue listening: they could tell him, for example, a few more things about his mother and her supposed illness, or about where she kept her savings bonds, or about Harry and about that golden centaur, not a bad sort really, but easily manipulated, and about who was manipulating him,

"I couldn't care less about any of that," said Ireneo,

"Well, you should,"

"Go on talking if it makes you happy,"

"It does," said the shoes, "You've put your finger right on it, it makes us extremely happy to talk, we almost can't stand not to,"

"You never spoke in the old days,"

"We spoke all the time, you just weren't ready to hear us,"

"That sounds like tawdry psychodrama talk,"

"Which doesn't make it invalid,"

"No, just insufferable,"

"You wound us,"

"I doubt it,"

"You are right to doubt, after all it is doubt that leads straight to the heart of error and out the other side—where are we going?"

"There is no 'we' here, it's just me and my shoes, out for a run, heading for the beach, la, la, la," and it was certainly true that Ireneo was making for the beach, but at the last minute, almost in spite of himself, he turned and climbed up one of the high streets that led, by way of wildly interlacing cobblestone streets, to a series of vista points of the bay, including the very cliff mentioned a moment ago, which during the springtime was covered with innumerable white and yellow daffodils, and that now was an immense emerald lawn bordered by a white gravel path and low slate wall, which the shoes said they admired and which Ireneo, almost sprinting, bore down on, as if he meant to leap off it and soar into space, and put an early end, as it were, to the day, and as he got closer and closer the shoes kept talking about the wall and masonry and the masons that had worked on this one and what a bunch of crooks they had been even if they had done nice work, and so when Ireneo swerved at the last minute and deftly sent, instead of himself, the shoes sailing over the wall and out into space, they were still going on about crooks and the corrupt, ancient art of wall building, though one may suppose that as they stopped climbing and started falling, out of this story and into some other, they switched topics, which was what Ireneo, heaving a little after his exertion but satisfied that he had performed his civic duty by disposing of the shoes where no one else could easily pick them up and put them on and more importantly where, should he become tempted, he would have a very hard, not to say impossible time finding them again, now hoped it would be possible for him to do, although the first order of business would be to acquire some replacement footwear, as the sidewalk and street beyond the green lawn sparkled with glass and streaks of oil against which his thin running socks and even thinner soles would be no defense at all.

AFTER SPENDING TIME ON THE BED, HARRY AND SOLANGE spent time at Harry's kitchen table, where, over a few bites of this and that pulled out of Harry's small refrigerator, Harry asked Solange to say a little more about the Lucite, he hadn't quite grasped her interest in deploying it, that substance in particular, and she said that while she hardly understood it any longer herself, the initial impulse had come from a story she had partially overheard as she had leaned one morning against a palm tree and looked out to sea and considered walking into it and contriving not to return, whereupon two old women with thick ankles came and plunked themselves down near her and one told the other a story that she had read in a romantic novel of some sort, and had not approved of, about a boat builder who had lost his beloved wife after a protracted illness and who, in his grief, thinking of the amber pendant she had always worn in which an ant, dead millions of years, had been marvelously preserved, had given such serious consideration to plunging first her remains and then himself in the Lucite solution he used to coat the hulls of his boats that he had gone so far as to set her body on his workbench and to look for a proper receptacle, but as he did this, it seemed to him he felt a hand descend on his shoulder and a voice, *her* voice, whisper in his ear, that his grief was betraying him, and that he should stop and go and announce her death to the authorities and see to a proper burial, and that if he did this, she would come and visit him in his dreams, wearing his favorite dress, a promise Solange had not been able to hear if she had kept, and while all she had left of her young man were scraps, she had immediately gotten hold of some Lucite and begun encasing what she had, not in hopes of provoking an analogous response, she was too grief-stricken to hope for anything, but because—and it was this impulse that had driven her out to the beach in the first place—she had suddenly been overcome by an urge to devour the little pile of bits and pieces she had left of him—which had led her to wonder with horror what she would have done had his entire body been there—to pluck them up and drop them into her mouth, and while that unbidden impulse had remained as she set to work encasing the bits of knife metal in Lucite, it grew less acute over the coming weeks and before long seemed to have vanished altogether,

"Though of course nothing like that ever really vanishes," Solange said,

"No it certainly doesn't," Harry said, and after they had sat silently gazing out over the sun-burnished rooftops around them, he added that while in this particular instance he was not in a position to empathize, he had heard of such cases, notably one involving a Buddhist monk, who had been unable to bear the thought of his dead lover's body being given up to the flames or to the perceived ignominy of decomposition, and had consequently, presumably because no quieting hand had come down on his shoulder, eaten the body, an act that had, according to the story, cursed him, though Harry couldn't say whether or not such an eventuality was merited,

"What happened to him?" Solange asked,

"He lived for many years as a madman in the ruins of his own monastery,"

"Then I'm glad that in the end I only nibbled on the end of one of my young man's shoelaces."

SOLANGE AND HARRY EMERGED FROM THE LATTER'S APART-
ment contentedly aware that their exchange of confi-
dences, no matter how satisfyingly thorough, could
reasonably be thought of as no more than an additional
incipit in what—barring any unforeseen accelerant—would
require a whole cascading series in order to move them
toward that something they had not, during their discussion of the matter, been quite willing to articulate, though
we might reasonably infer that the potential of an intense
acquaintance bolstered by duration was under discussion,
meaning that high spirits were the order of the evening as
they set off for the boulevard to recuperate and stow away
Solange's silver costume and Harry's Yellow Submarine
before heading together, as they had agreed, to the café to
have a light meal and a bottle or two of sparkling water
ahead of the revelations to come, though when they passed
the second floor door marked "Rubinski" their steps slowed
and they exchanged glances, but a collective shrug seemed
to take care of the matter for both of them and instead of
further discussing ghosts as they walked they turned to the
related but generally less noxious subject of dreams, for
Solange had had a corker the previous night, a nacreous
haze that had ended with a question, "What word do we
use to indicate that tame lions are living among us?" while
Harry had found himself in a landscape dotted with amal-
gamators on a walking tour led by a kind of magician

whose face, the dream had proposed to him, was "shining like a wet sword," and while neither Solange nor Harry was interested in digging around for submerged meaning in these dreams, they both found the inclusion of moments of language amidst the standard swarm of images strangely appealing, and no doubt would have found their way into an interesting conversation thereon as they gathered their things on the boulevard if Alfonso, still in full regalia, including his sword and hind legs, hadn't been waiting, arms crossed over his armored chest, next to the submarine,

"Our gondoleer," Harry said,

"He doesn't look happy," Solange said,

"You're right, he's not, he's been standing here waiting for three quarters of an hour next to this abandoned, borrowed Yellow Submarine waiting to see if the person who borrowed it from him would turn up again," Alfonso said sternly, while inwardly in fact he was quite pleased that Harry's negligence in re the submarine had so conveniently handed him a straightforward justification for rescinding Harry's occupational privileges, and he was preparing to broach this subject, and to extract an imminent date and time for Harry to fulfill his end of the bargain and tell him his story, which would no doubt intersect intriguingly with the connoisseurs planned attentions, when a curious thought, one that had not entered into his calculations about the source of his misgiving earlier, entered his mind—no doubt by some side door or other, the handle of which was Solange's happily smudged silver face or Harry's sweat-streaked wrists or the half-shredded sparkling water bottle splayed across the roots of the oak tree that rose and spread just behind them—and made him uncross his arms and recross them then look off to the side to study the thought again then once more before confirming that, yes, while of course as he well knew he had been the one who had told a certain handsome young man interested in taking up the living statue profession and who had come and stood in front of him, for the purpose of observation, for several days, that he might, since he was interested in golden things, just as well go and observe the technique of the angel near the top of the boulevard, and then of course a few days later the young man had become the golden angel's young man and then, some weeks later, had died horribly and smashed her heart to smithereens, all this he knew, but it hadn't occurred to him until just that very moment that it was the connoisseurs who had planted the suggestion in his mind, during one of their circuits, as they passed behind him, "Send that guy off to see Solange, that's who he ought to see next, that would be good, don't you think?" or had it been them? was he remembering something that had actually occurred or dropping depth charges from the present into the past? he didn't think so, and because he didn't, because there was doubt in his mind and maybe just a little more than doubt, especially given the expressions that had played over the connoisseurs' faces when they had discussed Harry earlier, instead of telling Harry it was time for him and the submarine to part ways, he leaned over, opened the hatch, and said,

"Climb in,"

"We're going somewhere," Harry said,

"I'll take you," Alfonso said,

"You're sure?" Solange said,

Alfonso patted the side of the submarine and said it would be good exercise,

"Are you going to take that stuff off or walk with it?" Harry said, pointing at Alfonso's hind legs,

"They're on rollers, they work even better than the submarine, every now and again I like to move around a little when I'm performing, it wouldn't do to walk off without my legs," Alfonso said, and before Harry could say something else, Solange took his arm and pulled him into the submarine and shut the hatch behind them, and after she had instructed Alfonso to grab her gear then told him where they were going, they were off, and as they moved off, Harry and Solange looked at each other and Solange said,

"I think he's going to tell us something,"

"I think so too," Harry said,

"The thing is I can't," Alfonso said, "Or at the very least I shouldn't, it's difficult, even tedious, extremely tedious, it's just that a moment ago I had a thought and that thought, well, made me think,"

"I thought a thought but the thought I thought was not the thought that I thought I thought," said Harry,

"If only," said Alfonso,

"This is about the connoisseurs, something to do with them, isn't it?" said Solange,

"It might and it might not be," said Alfonso,

"We saw you at the market with them earlier,"

"We had breakfast,"

"After the long night,"

"It was a long night, wasn't it, too long, maybe I'm just overtired,"

"Maybe we all are, I'm not finding this submarine as comfortable today as I used to, plus I saw a ghost," said Harry,

"Actually, I don't feel particularly tired," said Solange, "And when I saw you four this morning I got the feeling you were cooking something up, though I wouldn't have thought it had anything to do with us,"

"Well, ha, ha," said Alfonso,

"What's that supposed to mean?"

"I don't know, I really don't, look, just whatever it is you're going to do, don't do it,"

"You mean don't have dinner?"

"He means don't go with Ireneo, that is what you mean isn't it?"

"Who's Ireneo?"

"Some guy,"

"Some guy that was looking for you?"

"Why?"

"I forgot to mention it but he asked me about you,"

"What did you tell him?"

"I sent him goose chasing,"

"He got tired of chasing gooses and came to see me, but anyway, why shouldn't we go with Ireneo?"

"I didn't say you shouldn't go with anyone, I just said whatever it is you're going to do, don't do it,"

"The café is just over there," said Harry,

"Fine," said Alfonso, "I've warned you, which is a lot more than I should have done, though as a last thing I'll just say that I really don't have any idea if following my warning will help,"

"Fabulous," said Harry, "Thanks a billion,"

"Yes, that's not all that helpful, Alfonso," said Solange,

"Apologies, but that's all I can offer, I'm not sure if I knew more I would tell you, in fact I think I wouldn't, there may already be consequences, though I hope not, and now I'll have to go, and if you don't mind, Harry, I'll take the submarine along with me, you won't be needing it any-more will you?"

"No," said Harry,

"Good," said Alfonso, then he opened the hatch and Solange and Harry stepped out and went straight into the café and sat down at a table and ordered dinner and when dinner arrived, Harry said,

"Do you still want to go?"

"Yes, how about you?"

"Yes,"

"You have to admit that was a little odd,"

"Yes," Harry said, and shuddered, which made Solange shiver, about which they both laughed, then Ireneo arrived, bowed to Solange and apologized, in some detail, for the earlier misunderstanding that had kept her from her audi-ence with Doña Eulalia, told Harry that he was feeling just fine and that he had taken care of the issue that had made it seem, when they had spoken, like there was a problem, to whit he had thrown his shoes off a cliff and purchased the relatively quiet espadrilles he was wearing and wouldn't be doing any further running for the foreseeable future, then guided them off along what proved to be a fairly unproblematic set of twists and turns that ended in front of Doña Eulalia's building, and although Harry couldn't for the life of him understand why he hadn't been able to find said building when he had gone looking, he had the feeling that if he mentioned this to Ireneo, Ireneo would come up with something as bizarre and unexplained/unexplainable as he had about his shoes, and Harry, feeling more than a little fatigued, thought he would leave any additional ellipses to Doña Eulalia and her lamps, though Solange, perhaps because she felt much less implicated than Harry in what was to come next, felt no need whatsoever to keep quiet, and, because she had had her interest piqued, as they approached the large green door, said, "I'm walking in between someone who saw a ghost this morning and some-one else who felt he needed to throw his shoes off a cliff this afternoon—I know something about the ghost but nothing about the shoes, care to enlighten me?"

"No," Ireneo said, and if he spoke to Solange a little sharply, all the better as far as he was concerned, for it had cost him enough just to bring it all up for the purpose of clarifying his earlier behavior—Harry must have thought he looked "completely crackers," as his mother had liked to put it when he threw tantrums as a child—and even just the thought of the whole business was enough to make his throat go dry and the back of his neck tingle like someone had struck him sharply on one of the upper vertebrae with the sort of rubber mallets doctors used to test reflexes, or at least that was the way he had felt when, after leaving the little store wearing his new espadrilles, the feeling had presented itself and obliged him to turn around, climb the hill he had just made it back down, cross the emerald lawn once again and go and look out over the wall, first at the horror of gray clouds spreading across the far horizon, then at the disaster of blue below, then decide he'd better throw himself off it, whereupon he had placed both hands on the low wall and started to lift one of his feet and said to himself, "Good, it has all been tedious and baffling anyway," lifted his other foot onto the wall, looked at his unkempt toes and thought, "Good god those need trimming," and tensed to spring, only at that moment something stirred in his peripheral vision, something moving slowly toward him, something that was whistling an air so exasperating that it reminded him of stale coffee beans being put through a hand grinder, then of someone kicking in a glass display case, then of the taste of gasoline-soaked cardboard, then of where he was, teetering on the edge of a wall with a 500-foot drop, and then the something—three old men walking shoulder to shoulder along the gravel path—stopped whistling and one of these three old men said,

"It's just a pair of shoes,"

and another of them said,

"You don't need those things, don't be an idiot,"

then the whistling had recommenced and the three old men passed behind him, and the other half of his peripheral vision was engaged and just as it clicked on he thought he heard, somewhere amid the whistling, one of them say,

"Go and pick up Harry and take him where he's supposed to go,"

and then he had fallen over backwards off the wall and had lain on the path they had traversed and at first it seemed to him that the path was like a piece of ice and that it would be damaging to continue to lie there on it looking up at the clouds and the occasional bird slicing through the air, that his skin would stick to it and be torn off when he tried to stand, that he would find himself partially flayed, and as he thought this the whistling started up in his head as if he had put on earphones and hit play and this time it sounded to him like teeth breaking as they were directed by their owner to bite down on chunks of aggregate mineral, and in the meantime the feeling in the back of his neck returned and he wanted nothing more than to stand up and fling himself off the cliff, but he knew that if he did so he would tear off his skin and that as he fell through space he would fall in a great shower of blood, and he knew this long after he had realized that the ground was not cold in the slightest and that the whistling had stopped and that he was not going to throw himself off the cliff, and knowing it he stood and brushed the dust off of his back and smiled in what he was quite sure was not at all a reassuring manner at a woman who was standing on the green lawn petting an obese German shepherd and staring nervously at him, and then he had stopped knowing it in quite such a debilitating manner and had started off again down the hill and had not paused, except to buy a bottle of water and a large packet of paprika-spiced fried minnows from a vendor near the harbor, which he shoved by the handful into his mouth until the packet was empty and he had calmed down enough to find a public restroom and wash his face and run damp fingers through his hair, before proceeding to his rendezvous, where he had hoped to preempt any questions to do with the shoes, a strategy that had worked quite well with Harry, but not, alas, with Solange, who nevertheless, far from taking visible offense at his curt answer, reached out, put her hand on his forearm and held it there until it occurred to him not only that he had been shaking, but also that he had now stopped,

"It has been a very long day," he said, giving a little bow and turning away to cover the fact that he had gone quite crimson, and as he left them in the courtyard to go and let Doña Eulalia know, as she had asked him to, that they had arrived, his blush deepened and the tingling in the back of his neck returned, as did the shaking, and it was only with the greatest effort that he made it inside and up the short flight of stairs to Doña Eulalia's room, where he leaned his head against the cool, reassuring wood of the door and said,

"I've brought them."

As they stood in the courtyard waiting for Ireneo to reappear, Harry had more than enough time to remark that the circumstances surrounding this current visit differed in more than one way from those surrounding the last, and he had to admit, he told Solange, that he was disappointed that they had not been immediately led into a room full of mysterious individuals dressed in black and so forth, but Solange gave no clear indication that she had heard him so Harry busied himself with kicking at the dirty cobblestones, counting the coins in his pockets, looking up at the square of dark sky that loomed above them and wondering if he had eaten his dinner—a pork cutlet and some mashed yams sprinkled with fish flakes—too quickly or drunk too much sparkling water and otherwise attempted to keep his mind off ghosts, possibly treacherous golden centaurs, old guys who made his companion shiver because, as she had told him that afternoon after they had exchanged stories, of the way she had caught them all smiling horribly as they stood behind her one recent afternoon whispering about how sorry they were about her loss, etc., his own tendency to shudder, as he put it to himself, rather than shiver, a distinction Solange had said she found very interesting and wanted to explore during their next tête-à-tête, and guides who threw their shoes off cliffs in the middle of the day then acted unpleasant about it afterwards . . . convinced that if he let his mind go in their direction he would find himself off on a journey whose futility would only be exceeded by its unpleasantness, a formula which, to his annoyance, got stuck in his mind and played over and over again like, he thought looking back up at the indigo sky, the perfect description not just of his life over the past decade, but of his entire being, this thing that he had once described in one of many terrible love poems as an incandescent bulb that had come on and would not go out, even if someone smashed it, so much for that, at least in the case of his former wife, who had left him long before it had happened and had not blamed him or at least not too harshly, but he had to admit that he was not unhappy to be reminded, as he cast a glance over at Solange, that it was still capable of illumination, that it wasn't, after all, quite as irrevocably cold as the Neptunists had once contended the interior of the earth was, that it still, that *he* still, had some life left in him as the hackneyed expression went,

"You know," Solange said, breaking into his thoughts, "Ireneo looked more like he had seen a ghost than you did," an assertion with which Harry found he wholeheartedly agreed and—because the gap between the previous apparently unflappable Ireneo of that first night and the one who had looked a moment ago like he might burst into tears seemed so enormous—was troubled by and thought to respond to, only at the moment he started to say, "He did, didn't he,"

the individual in question, immense turquoise eyes seeming to float in front of him, came back out through the door he had disappeared through looking even more crazed than he had previously, no doubt in part because his head and upper torso were now sopping wet, but he shed no more light on this change in disposition than he had on the business of the shoes, nor did he say anything when Harry asked if they were now going to go into the room with the people and the lamps, and a moment later they found themselves sitting in a conventionally lit parlor of sorts in comfortable purple velvet armchairs with a beaming old woman dressed in a powder-blue pantsuit and improbably high heels, who offered them tea, which they accepted, then lemon-filled ginger cookies, which they declined, at which juncture Ireneo, who had been dripping away next to a sort of curio cabinet filled with odds and ends of all shape and variety, frowned and left the room—to spend the rest of what was to prove a very long, cold night fighting the urge to go back up to the cliff and kill himself—and Doña Eulalia said,

"Excellent, I am so glad you are both here," a remark that was so far from being a mere nicety that she felt compelled to repeat it, this time laying the stress on the word "both," for if she had been absolutely incapable of keeping this Harry and the unpleasantness that lay in store for him from her thoughts for more than a few seconds over the past several days, his companion, whose face Doña Eulalia could see had until recently been very broken indeed, had been more on her mind than she would have thought justified, given that, as best she could tell, anything that might until recently have required a candle and concomitant consideration had moved on, but as the specifics of the cases she was drawn to were, as we have seen, rarely her forte—so much so that it had dawned on her after she told Ireneo to go and ask the centaur where Harry was that she must have picked up the information from elsewhere, possibly Ireneo's blasted shoes—she smiled at Solange, echoed Ireneo's apology, and contented herself with saying that, as she, Solange, had clearly sensed herself, her loved one had moved on and was at peace, as she could now be, which, Doña Eulalia thought, was true, for now at any rate, and the limited parameters of "for now," in Solange's only mildly alarming case, struck her as sufficient, especially since contact had been reestablished in such a satisfactory way—in fact, she would have to ask them both to leave their cards or if they didn't have cards, of course they probably didn't, at least their phone numbers, so that any eventual follow-up protocols could be observed, which, who knew, might prove even more necessary in the case of Solange than Harry, though she doubted it, she highly doubted it—and with that in mind she reached for one of the ginger lemon cookies and put the whole thing into her mouth, crushing it with her tongue against the roof of her mouth in the way she was accustomed to and that always gave her great satisfaction, and she might have put another one in straight after the first if Harry, who until that moment had been sitting silently next to Solange, hadn't looked around the room, made a sort of clicking sound then asked,

"Why don't you have a lamp on your head and aren't you supposed to hum or something?"

"Ah yes, well, different circumstances, different modes of transmission," said Doña Eulalia, licking around in one of the gaps in her teeth for some remaining lemon crème and thinking, good god I must come off like a complete and utter charlatan,

"Oh," said Harry, sounding a little deflated, as if by his question he had hoped to elicit an indication that even though they weren't in the big room downstairs with her nincompoop relations at any moment the lights above them would go off and the lamps would come out and the furniture would start shaking or something like that, a speculation that diverged only in the matter of the shaking furniture from the actual thought that had run not just through Harry's mind, but Solange's as well, causing her, Solange, to raise an eyebrow and fix Doña Eulalia with a quizzical gaze this latter found so noteworthy that when a moment later she left off looking around in her mouth for more lemon crème, leaned forward, tapped Harry's knee twice, cleared her throat, and said, "They're coming," she almost couldn't refrain from turning to Solange and adding, "For both of you."

AFTER RATHER FEEBLY, SHE THOUGHT, POINTING HER FINGER at the door and watching, through half-closed eyes, Harry and Solange make their way through it, Doña Eulalia took a deep breath, reached for the teapot, and, suddenly aware, in the way that these things came to her, that her night was not yet over, drank directly from its spout, then asked herself aloud what situation she would have the opportunity to mishandle next, and, still aloud, whether she ought not to go and get one of the lampshades from the reception hall downstairs, put it on her head, roll back her eyeballs and hum, though in the event she had so little time to wait that were she to have acted on this self-mocking impulse she would barely have made it halfway down the back stairs before the second round of visitors appeared, as it was, the chill that preceded them, as they stood waiting on the other side of the main door to her bedroom, after having gotten into the house she certainly didn't know how, was such that she reached for one of her woolen throws and pulled it up to her chin before taking another deep voice and calling out that the door was open,

"Of course it is," said one of the three old men she found standing in front of her a moment later,

"It's always open, your door, isn't it?" said another,

"It all just drifts right in, kind of like a walkie-talkie without an off switch, although maybe the reception isn't so good," said the third,

"Won't you gentlemen sit down," said Doña Eulalia, folding her arms around herself and crossing her ankles, "You will forgive me if I don't stand,"

"Oh sure we'll forgive you,"

"We just love to forgive,"

"But we won't sit, standing seeming preferable,"

"Keeping the blood flowing,"

"Through our old bones,"

"Are you cold, Doña Eulalia, you look cold if you don't mind my saying so . . ."

"You three brought a chill in with you,"

"Which we don't always do,"

"Sometimes we bring in the opposite,"

"Light up the night, heat up the party,"

Doña Eulalia looked from one to the other of them and saw nothing except old men with watery eyes wearing sweaters and windbreakers,

"Your powers fail you,"

"You draw a blank,"

"Gaze upon the void,"

"It would not, gentlemen, be the first time,"

"Or the last, right?"

"How can I help the three of you?"

"Oh you've already helped us,"

"We're grateful,"

"Here to express our gratitude,"

"We brought you a token,"

"Some chocolate,"

"Easily edible water fowl,"

"Custom made,"

"Just marvelous,"

"It's about Harry," said Doña Eulalia, looking, without moving, at the ribbon-wrapped box one of her visitors was holding, "Or perhaps it's about his friend,"

"For someone so chilled you're awfully warm,"

"Or it's about my Ireneo, you're the ones who gave him a fright, earlier today,"

"Your Ireneo, I like that, it has a nice ring,"

"We just told him it wasn't worth going looking for those shoes,"

"That he had better things to do,"

"We helped him,"

"Who are you?"

"Who are we?"

"I love it,"

"You tell us,"

"I see," said Doña Eulalia, still looking at the box, which was now sitting next to her teapot, its cargo of what looked like chocolate ducklings on clear display through its plastic top,

"It's going to get colder tonight,"

"A turn in the weather,"

"Drink tea and eat chocolate, it will keep you toasty,"

"That's what they do in the Amazon,"

"Something like that,"

"When they get a fever,"

"Or take fright,"

"Being as it never really gets cold there,"

"Anyway, we won't keep you,"

"We just stopped by to deliver the token,"

"The mark of our gratitude,"

"Have one,"

"I should have warned them, poor dears,"
"Oh, you've warned them,"
"You've been marvelous,"
"Now you deserve a rest, a good sleep,"
"Have a chocolate, they're excellent,"
"I don't think so," said Doña Eulalia,
"But we do," said one of the old men,
"Yes, we certainly do," said one of the others,
"We certainly fucking do."

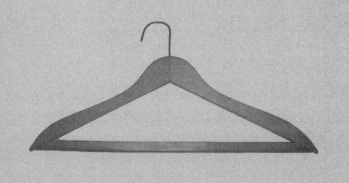

III

In the places
only the dead dream, I will look for our reflections.

THAT NIGHT SOMETHING LIKE A WIND LEFT OVER FROM deepest winter made its way through the city, banging shutters, frosting balconies, flattening exposed strips of grass, crisping flowers, scattering wadded paper and ice cream wrappers and freshly discarded metal cans, and making the people who were still out, everywhere—their eyes scanning the heavily mitigated darkness for directional cues that would simultaneously lead them further into adventure and help them avoid disaster—wrap goose-pimpled arms around themselves and reach for coats they weren't even sure they could have found if they were at home, and while it would be maudlin to propose a direct connection between that wind—which among many other things simultaneously rekindled then extinguished the end of the perambulating Raimon's real cigar and froze the tips and knuckles of his strange hands, smashed the hat off the balding and unusually delicate head of Almundo, of Almundo's Store for Living Statues, as he closed up for the night, and elicited an extraordinarily general and multilingual polyphony of "What the Fucks"—and Doña Eulalia's message, it would be needlessly artificial not to pause for a moment in the insistent face of it and let it stretch its serpentine fingers through the groaning city, through its parks and plazas, its courtyards and late-night kiosks, before returning to Harry—an earlier incarnation thereof—reading the paper a lifetime ago on a stone terrace that looked out over an immense caldera whose rippling waters sparked and glittered in an afternoon light so ferocious it seemed to him, as he told Solange long after they had left Doña Eulalia's, when his voice had finally returned, an exact inverse of the icy howling that had kept them up half the night under inadequate covers, one that would sear his flesh, char his bones, and leave nothing behind but a few black crumbs for the young waiter to sweep up, which was really neither here nor there, because, he said, what he had thought of in particular when Doña Eulalia had made her pronouncement then, politely but firmly, told them to leave without asking any questions because they would not, because they *could not,* be answered, was not of the temperature, but rather of the palm reader, festooned with purple and turquoise scarves, as well as some kind of Kung Fu jacket, who had been working her way from table to table across the terrace until, inevitably, she had appeared before him and none-too-politely demanded his hand, which he had surprised himself by removing from the top left corner of the paper and offering to her, though without quite looking away from the article he was perusing as he did this— which, he told Solange, had been meant to indicate a measure of disinterest in or even disdain for the proceedings—but before his disdain had had a chance to fully unfurl, the palm reader had given out a shriek, flung his hand away, and moved off so quickly that she was gone before he could take his eyes off the paper, and because his eyes were more or less there anyway, and the thought of someone looking at his hand and shrieking was unsettling, he had continued to pretend to read, until, after not too terribly long, he had been able to actually continue reading and enjoying the view of the caldera, if not the infernal heat, and then his time alone had ended and the others had joined him, and while in the ensuing avalanche of activity he had stopped thinking about the palm reader and her reaction to his palm, that night he had seen her billowing scarves and Kung Fu jacket and heard her shriek over and over again and then, less than a year later, well . . .

YES, WELL, HARRY THOUGHT, TRYING, WITHOUT MUCH LUCK, to swallow and realizing that he had been sleeping, that he had finally dreamed his way out of the misery of the cold, and that, of course, Solange was no longer there, that he would not see her, if at all—and given his behavior the *if* was not inconsiderable—until later in the day, that for the past few minutes he had been telling his sad little story to himself, a recitation he had punctuated by smacking the silver bell, then grabbing it and without quite knowing why shoving it into his pocket, and that, to carry matters to a head, as one might say, there was now a knocking at his door, like a reification of Doña Eulalia's portentous words, and for several seconds he lay under his covers without moving, until it suddenly seemed imperative that he move, and quickly, before whoever it was stopped knocking and went away, just in case it was, well, *them,* so he leapt up, ran his fingers through his disastrous hair and, still trying to swallow, his heart smashing itself against his ribs, ripped opened the door, though not onto any unspecified "They," but rather onto a clearly distraught Señora Rubinski, who told him he must come down to her apartment immediately because her husband, Señor Rubinski, was not well,

"Not well," Harry repeated, trying and failing to catch his breath,

"He won't come out of his bath," Señora Rubinski said and, taking Harry by the wrist, led him downstairs, through her front door, over the recently polished wide-plank floorboards of a long hallway, through a living room glowing in the morning light coming in through gauzy drapes, and down another, longer hallway to a door covered in chipped blue paint that stood slightly ajar,

"In there," Señora Rubinski said,

"But it's not locked," Harry said,

"I never said it was locked,"

"I assumed . . ."

"I don't follow you,"

"But you haven't gone in?"

"Into my husband's bath, without his permission . . ." Señora Rubinski gave out a snort of indignation and Harry, rather hopeful that the wind was still howling and he was still dreaming, nodded gravely to show that he understood and endorsed the local protocol, knocked lightly on the door, said, "Excuse me, Señor Rubinski, it's me, Harry Tichborne, your neighbor," then stepped in.

THERE WAS SO MUCH STEAM AND SO LITTLE LIGHT IN THE Rubinski's bathroom that it took Harry, who initially had a hard time pulling his eyes up off the black and white tiles covering the floor, a good while to get his bearings, and a good while longer to register that the source of all the steam, an enormous, claw-footed white bathtub, which sat a luxurious distance from the door, was to all appearances empty, but given the circumstances, i.e. the presumed condition of its presumed inhabitant, he thought it prudent to wait until he could be absolutely sure before making his report to Señora Rubinski, so that when this latter called in to ask if everything was all right, Harry said that it was *as far as he could tell,* an absurd response that nevertheless seemed to satisfy the Señora, who said nothing further as Harry crept over and, nervously fingering the bell in his pocket, peered into the bathtub and, through the steam and gray residue of what might have been bubbles, its considerable depths, then, after checking in the room's closet, where he found only a moth-chewed raincoat, made out of the most extraordinary purple cloth, which made him think again of the palm reader and look rather mournfully down at his hand, he went and sat on a sturdy wooden box placed between the sink and the tub, whispered, "I'm just going to sit here for a few minutes in case you are here and I can be of any service, Señor Rubinski," and while there was no answer, at least none that Harry recognized, he continued to sit there and, in the voluptuous warmth enveloping him, so pleasant after the long, cold night that had left him so tired and more than a little out of sorts, even let his eyes shut and his mind wander to the past, by the palm reader and the newspaper to the caldera, which dwarfed the great ocean liners that entered it and seemed never to stop glittering, even at night, when clouds covered the moon and stars and he and his family huddled together in the big bed, and his darlings demanded stories about the gods who had stolen children and the mortals who had longed for their return, which now, as he sat in the Rubinski's bathroom with his eyes shut, seemed to have everything in the world to do with the way his heart had started smashing at the knock on his door, not to mention the totally inadequate farewell which had been all he had been capable of offering Solange when—after he had told her he really had no idea who the "They" in question might be, not once but, after she had very gently, very delicately, asked him again, twice—she had left him, saddened and perhaps even angry he thought, to return to her own apartment, ostensibly to make sure her windows were shut, but more likely because of the lie he had so shamelessly let out into the room, a nasty little cloud of razors and butterflies that had swirled between them for the rest of the time she had stayed, both of them well aware, Harry was sure, that unlike the small one Solange had told as they lay next to each other in the Yellow Submarine this was a significant lie, one that if not confessed to could end up shredding whatever it was that was occurring between them, but rather than make what would have been a straightforward, expedient correction, Harry had simply watched it swirl around the room and, even when Solange had offered him an opening, a "perhaps you'd rather not talk about it, I completely understand," had said nothing and eventually Solange had left, and he had gone on watching it and sticking his hand into it whenever it passed, and sometime during the night it had tired of moving around the room and had leapt back into his throat, and when it did so Harry realized that by making no effort at all to chase it out of the room while Solange had still been there he had done something very foolish, potentially damaging, and to what purpose? he had wondered, before going into the long story, the story he had both dreamed and told himself, about the palm reader, before Señora Rubinski had started pounding on the door, and Harry, his heart smashing against his ribs, had ripped it open, very much hoping that They had arrived, had come back, had returned, had accomplished what he had spent years hoping they would, just like Señor Rubinski, exactly like Señor Rubinski who had returned to make himself available for morning and evening walks, or like the calming hand placed on the shoulder of the crazed boat builder who wanted to plunge his lost love into Lucite, but They hadn't, and outside of his hopes he couldn't even be sure who or what "They" referred to, or even if Doña Eulalia was anything other than a crank of the first order with her lemon cookies and lamps, but the fact remained that there was only one "They" worth mentioning, insofar as he was concerned, and what would it have hurt him to say it, what could it have hurt to tell Solange, what could anything, he thought, now hurt and yet here he was, hurting, waiting for the warm steam to convert itself into the cold, dark water that the presence of Solange, whom he had chased away with his lies, had been keeping at bay, and when he pressed his hands against his lips and opened his eyes, Señor Rubinski, his stringy hair plastered to the top of his dripping, greenish head, was smiling over the edge of the tub at him, "I died in an industrial accident, fell into the paper mill where I worked, was torn to pieces," he said.

HARRY ONCE TOOK AND DID POORLY IN A COURSE IN ELE-
mentary logic, and while apart from the gross outline
of a few riddles involving knights and knaves, which as we
have seen had become one of the weapons in his fights
against his legs, very little of the content of the course now
remained with him, and as he sat in the steamy bathroom
and stared into Señor Rubinski's unblinking black eyes, he
found himself thinking of Wittgenstein's "Whereof we cannot speak, thereof we must remain silent," which his pro-
fessor had scrawled on the board at the end of the course
as a kind of flourish, an assertion that seemed to buttress
the decision that he, Harry, had taken, if decision it could
be called, to suck in his lips and hold them pinched
between his teeth as Señor Rubinski first cleared his throat,
then coughed, then begged Harry's pardon, then began
again to speak, and since Harry, suddenly feeling completely unequal to the circumstance, jammed his hand
against the bell in his pocket and more or less pinched his
mind along with his lips between his teeth during the
lengthy opening movement of Señor Rubinski's speech,
which, for the record, had evoked the multiple vectors the
minor—that was to say lost or unaccounted for—bits of his
flesh and cloth and bone had taken while pinwheeling their
way across the shop as the machine "gleefully prosecuted
his demise," we might be excused for leaving him long
enough to observe that unlike the scraps of Señor Rubinski

that went sailing out higgledy-piggledy across his former place of work, a radical convergence, long flirted with, of the vectors being inscribed by the various major characters in Harry's life is now definitively underway: witness Ireneo, finally starting to warm up after a night spent chilled both in body—in his damp clothes—and in spirit—despite Doña Eulalia's efforts to clear his mind by pulling him into her bathroom and dumping a bucket of water over his head—eating octopus porridge at a stall near the beach while Solange, not nearly as negatively affected by Harry's lie as Harry imagines her to be, but unsettled by it—and by a highly unexpected incident about which more, in her own words, a little later—nonetheless, and consequently out walking as much to restore her circulation after a short night spent shivering in her apartment as to think things through, moves along a near-perfect line of fat palms toward him, though she is still some distance away when the connoisseurs, whose tune Ireneo has been attempting to call to mind as he gazes into the comforting mass of rice-flecked tentacles in the bowl before him, come up on either side of Ireneo and without saying a word convince him that he should take a little walk with them, which is the moment that Solange spots the four of them, shivers deeply, and 1) because in addition to worrying about Harry and whatever it is that is supposed to be coming for him or that he now thinks is coming for him and isn't ready to talk about, she has spent a good portion of the time since she last saw Ireneo wondering what became of him after he left Doña Eulalia's and 2) because the newly formed quartet looks from a distance much like the one formed by the connoisseurs and Alfonso at the market, decides immediately to follow them, which she sets about with a degree of theatricality she finds almost comical, as if it were the silver angel moving with fluent stiffness from palm tree to palm tree and occasionally pressing itself against the sides of the red roofed villas then high stone buildings they pass as they move into the city, even though the moving tableau before her strikes her as anything but amusing: in fact, she very quickly becomes convinced that Ireneo's confusion the night before must have involved the connoisseurs and, after shivering again, so hard this time that she thinks it might pass for one of Harry's shudders and has to stop and shut her eyes and count to ten before she can continue, she finds herself swept by a series of fierce urges: to call out to Ireneo, to tell him to come with her, to run away and find Harry, to see what the connoisseurs would do—these old bastards, she thinks, whom she has never liked, even when, in the early days, they used to bring her boxes of fresh oranges and chocolate squares and fish-shaped marzipan and little bundles of wood to burn in her fireplace, until out of embarrassment and an inability to reciprocate she asked them to stop, which they did, though not graciously, a good deal of grumbling was involved, of muttering, perhaps even threats—but before she can do anything, the four of them, who have not once looked back, have entered the front door of a building, an unusual one as it occurs, one of several similar structural anomalies scattered throughout the city that were designed by the sort of visionary/crackpot who every generation or so arises in great metropolises and pulls fistfuls of the future out of his pockets and smears them all over the present, with varying results, as in the case of this building, which has always looked to Solange when she has passed it and wondered who was moving behind its oddly shaped windows not so much like it is melting, as the widely available literature suggests, as drooling, *How curious that they went into that one,* Solange thinks, and then it strikes her that of course she knows who is really coming for Harry, not, as he was not prepared to tell her, his lost ones, but rather the old bastards, just as they came for Alfonso, for Ireneo, for—and here she shivers again—*her,* which was exactly, "for her," what Señor Rubinski said to Harry that at last made him release his mind and lips and sit up straight and listen, and so we will have to leave Solange's revelation hanging in the air and close this parenthetical although before we do so, before we return to Harry, who after all and for better or worse is the major and ever more central shareholder in his story, and give Señor Rubinski the floor, we might just observe that as Solange, now lost in thought, begins to put distance between herself and the building, Ireneo, who has already been dismissed—and the verb is chosen with care—by the connoisseurs, steps silently out of it, squints his turquoise eyes, sees her, and begins to follow.

"FOR HER, CERTAINLY, BUT ALSO FOR MYSELF," SEÑOR Rubinski said, "because let's be quite clear, being dead is infinitely less entertaining than even the quietest existence, for example the variety enjoyed by a midlevel supervisor in a paper plant whose greatest joy is the near silent dinners and walks and inconsequential domestic interludes he enjoys with his wife, the smell of sautéed minnows, the swirl of multicolored hats on the boulevard, the delicious clink of cranberry crystal being set down on a pewter tray, there is nothing to smell with down there, nothing to see with, nothing to hear, we simply feel and what we feel is not always so marvelous, and thus when they came to me, I said, so to speak, 'yes, I will do it,' and they took me to a large room lined, as I saw afterwards, with row upon row of hangers upon which hung the repaired remains of all those who they told me were there with me, and the number was so great that when they had me back in what one of them referred to inelegantly but not inaccurately as 'my drippings,' which looked not much the worse for wear, incidentally, for what they had been put through when I leaned too close to the shredder, I swooned a little to think of us all being stored in this way, with all of our remains kept on hand, a practicality which they explained after kicking me back to attention that greatly facilitated the sort of furlough that from time to time they granted so many of us, and then they kicked me again and without ceremony shoved me through a door that had been burned through the rough concrete wall and I found myself in the front room lying on the marvelous red velvet couch you must have walked past when my wife brought you in to join me and which I spent endless miraculous hours on before my ravishment, if you will permit a moment's fancy, by the shredder, not an instant of which I felt at the time, by the way, but all of which I have felt every—I underscore *every* moment since—regardless, there I was on the red velvet couch and then a moment later there was my poor wife, who after letting out a screech that, alas, quite neatly shattered the aforementioned cranberry glass pitcher and two out of four hourglasses from my old collection, came and knelt beside me and asked me if I had had a nice rest and then what would I like for the lunch she would begin preparing the minute we had returned from our walk, a walk I was none too eager to embark upon, being unsure of the viability, you see, of my drippings, but I had returned, as I said, in the main, for her, and so I allowed her to attempt to set a hat on my head, to whimper a little when it fell through me and onto the floor, to chatter a great deal at me about what seemed very little, and then to lead me downstairs and out onto the street, which is when I had the happy fortune of encountering you—happy not merely because of your kindness to my wife, during what she had described to me as her recent moments of doubt, but also because, and here we come to the crux of it, between the time that I had been stuffed, with very little ceremony I might add, back into my drippings and the moment I swooned, I noticed that on the short rack in the sort of dressing room they had me in there were a number of other drippings at the ready just next to the bloody hanger on which, I presumed, my own had been taken from, which would have meant very little at all except that after I swooned and before I came fully to, under the shower, so to speak, of their blows, I had the distinct impression that one of them said your name, Harry, and that the other laughed after he had said it, and while of course there are untold thousands of Harrys in the world, there have never, to my knowledge, been any others in my building, and so I said to myself when my wife mentioned you and then when we saw you, I must find a way to speak to this Harry, and to tell him what I have just told you,"

"*Drippings,*" Harry said,

"Yes, well it's rather unfortunate isn't it," Señor Rubinski said, "but when one has been on the other side, as it were, well, then it makes more sense, much more sense, I can't tell you, my dear Harry, just exactly how much good sense it makes, especially when you have seen the hangers, all of them, and what covers the floors, they must reconstitute themselves, the drippings, because there is so much of them on the floors, it was quite slippery, but I'm wandering, this was happening earlier with my wife, I'm afraid I gave her quite a turn talking about those floors, but it's a different matter once you've seen them, once you've been there, and know you must go back, I was lying here in my bath, greatly enjoying it when I fell asleep and was there again, and it was not a dream, no I don't think so, and when I woke there you were, I must have dozed for some time if my wife thought to get you, but you don't look well,"

"Don't I?" said Harry, who now wished very much indeed that he had managed to keep his lips and mind pinched shut, that he had put them in a vice and cranked it as tightly as it would go, and that he had shut his eyes and hadn't stared at Señor Rubinski, sitting there in his drippings, with one arm lolling over the side of the tub, "Drippings," Harry said again and found it quite curious that he didn't feel sick, that, unlike his reaction to Alfonso's story about Solange, he felt no need to excuse himself and lean over the sink and retch, or run out of the Rubinski's apartment, up to his own apartment and retch, to run out onto the street and retch, to run down the streets screaming and retching, to smash his head with a piece of brick and retch,

"Whose drippings were hanging on those hangers?" Harry said quietly, not needing to retch,

"I don't know, I thought you might," Señor Rubinski said,

"Well, I don't," said Harry, adding, "And I'm afraid that now, since I can see that you are all right, I'll have to go,"

"All right," said Señor Rubinski, "Yes, I suppose I am all right, yes, I suppose I am," whereupon Harry stood, and as he did it appeared to him that all there was to Señor Rubinski was what could be seen above the surface of the water, that there was nothing below—his lower drippings had deserted him,

"Good-bye," Harry said,

"I hope I've been helpful," Señor Rubinski said,

"Yes, quite, thank you, best of luck," Harry said, then stepped out of the bathroom, shut the door behind him, walked back down the long hallway and into the living room where he saw Señora Rubinski, asleep in an enormous green armchair pushed up close to the red couch, holding a damp, mauve handkerchief between two curled fingers, looking unnervingly like certain representations of martyred and jaundiced saints painted on one altarpiece after another during a particularly grim decade of the Northern Renaissance into which, during the early days of his despair, Harry had done no small amount of research, then, having decided not to attempt to disturb the image before him to make his report, that the drippings in the bathroom would find their way out to see the image if they wanted to, he went out the Rubinski's door, down the stairs, and into the warm sunlight, which gave a pleasant glow to the cobbled street, despite the presence, everywhere Harry looked, of so much wind-strewn debris.

S IGNIFICANT WEATHER EVENTS HAVE THE EFFECT OF ACCEL-erating the natural redistribution of the contents of cities, and even more so aseasonal events that play themselves out in population centers already so thoroughly given over to casually disseminating natural and artificial ephemera, so it was that first Solange and then Ireneo found themselves negotiating swirls and crescents of heavy sand and crushed palm frond blown half a mile inland, a suite of antique iron sconce lamps snapped off their rusting hinges, clouds of green glass, pieces of pastel-colored Styrofoam escaped, along with a packing order that ended up far out to sea, from a box swept off an oversized window ledge jutting from one of the many decrepit buildings perched in a crooked line along the city's eastern border, and seemingly endless sheets of brightly colored newspaper, including several aged blue sheets of a commemorative sports edition of one of the larger dailies, printed twenty-five years ago, lying in a puddle of glass, perhaps torn from the wall of a café that had left its doors open, Ireneo thought as he stepped past and wished for the 100th time since he had thrown them over the cliff that he had his running shoes back or at the very least something sturdier than these cheap espadrilles, which were comfortable enough for an afternoon at the beach, but not for the sort of mileage he had put on them as he wandered the frigid streets in his damp shirt, dealing with what Doña Eulalia had told him would feel and had felt much like a with-drawal—she had experienced it herself and for a period of some hours while it was occurring had had her husband strap her to the bed so that she wouldn't be tempted to attempt to retrieve her own treacherous shoes from the furnace or try to throw herself in after them, it was awful, she had said, noting that on top of his experience with the shoes, he had had another fright, had seen something, a speculation that Ireneo had neither contradicted nor affirmed, though he had let out a bit of a whistle that had made Doña Eulalia raise an eyebrow and say, "Ah," which is exactly what Ireneo had said when those three, as he had spent the night referring to the connoisseurs, had a few minutes before offered to employ him, had told him that a certain guy had let them down and that they had need of someone who knew the city and had experience in what they called *stuff,* and that if he was interested in what would be a strictly part-time gig, one that wouldn't conflict with his other obligations, he could start right this second by fol-lowing the angel, who was at this very moment standing outside the building on the street thinking about making a getaway that would sooner or later take her and conse-quently Ireneo to Harry, and when he, Ireneo, had found Harry, he could tell him to come and see them in this building, second floor, door on the right, and he would have fulfilled his first task,

"Interested?" one of them said,

"Ah," Ireneo said, but standing there with them was like standing, so the image came to him, in the center of one of those medieval maidens whose spiked doors would at any moment snap shut around him, and when one of

LAIRD HUNT :: 170

them lifted his arm to scratch something on his face, Ireneo did something he hadn't done very much of during his life, which is to say that he cringed, and they said,

"Good,"

and Ireneo,

"All right," and he left the courtyard where they had been standing and without great enthusiasm began to follow the angel, who by the by seemed to him rather small and pretty as she hurried along, looking in the sudden waves of sunlight extraordinarily unbroken, thoroughly, even from his vantage point, unlike she had when he had first seen her sitting in the wake of her own melancholy at the café—an observation that caused him to reflect, salubriously, on human resilience—and as he looked at her he sped up, at very nearly the same time that, the sense of urgency surrounding her rapid forward propagation having diminished, she slowed down, so that before very long—a few paces after Ireneo had stepped over the blue sports pages in fact—he cleared his throat and came up alongside Solange, who jumped a little, then shrugged, then smiled, and so they found themselves walking next to each other, with neither one, in the instance, too terribly surprised,

"I'm supposed to follow you," said Ireneo,

"I thought you worked for Doña Eulalia," said Solange,

"I do," said Ireneo, and as he said this it struck him that perhaps the "Ah" Doña Eulalia had uttered and that he had repeated, there before those three, had had some kind of prophylactic effect, after all it hadn't taken him very long to disobey them,

"Where are you going?" he said,

"Who's coming for him?" Solange said,

"I don't know,"

"Is it those three?"

"I don't know, I never know, just like I didn't know who you called us about,"

"She doesn't tell you?"

"She doesn't know either, she says it's like those images on radar, they more or less all look alike, she just has a sense of how close they are and where they're heading,"

"Radar?"

"Yes,"

"I see,"

"That's right,"

"Who is she?"

"Doña Eulalia? an old woman who sees things, the city is crawling with them, all cities probably are,"

"Can she help him?"

"It depends on what you mean by *help,* she's something of a generalist, she's mostly pretty indirect, but she can surprise you,"

"Have you ever worked with Lucite?"

Ireneo looked at her,

"It's used to encase things, enclose them, you have to wear gloves,"

"No, I haven't,"

"I lost someone very dear to me,"

"Yes, so I understand,"

"When my grief started leaving me, which it did far more quickly than I can see now that I was aware of, I started taking little bits and pieces of that person, of what was left of him, and burying them in clear plastic, there's a whole story that goes with it,"

"Indeed," Ireneo said,

"One that found its ending last night after I left Harry's and went home, would you like to hear that ending?"

"Yes,"

"One of my tears, which is to say a shard of metal caught in Lucite, spoke to me at some length as I was crossing the kitchen to go to bed, what do you think of that?"

"These are strange times,"

"They seem to grow stranger and stranger,"

"What did it say?"

"It said, in essence, that it no longer wished to be a tear,"

"Who could blame it,"

"That's more or less what I thought and how I responded and then it went quiet and I threw it and its fellows into the trash,"

"Which is where we all end up,"

"I think I'm going to go over to the boulevard and just stand there for a while,"

"Do you mind if I join you, I think I won't go and find Harry just now,"

"You could find him later, in fact, later, I'll probably go and see him and you can follow me then, if you still want to,"

"I'm not sure I will,"

"I like that Harry,"

"Yes,"

"I like him quite a bit, although it's probably hopeless, my liking him, what isn't?"

"Doña Eulalia had me light more than one candle for him,"

"Multiple blips on the radar screen?"

"Something like that,"

"You know those old bastards used to bring me candy,"

"Candy?"

"Boxes and boxes, like they were after my teeth, wanted them to rot and fall out,"

"Doña Eulalia said he, Harry, was like a well that had sprung a leak, and that it would likely be hard to find a way to plug it,"

"I feel a little like a well that's sprung a leak,"

"I could tell you about my shoes,"

"Yes, and the cliff,"

"I'll think about Harry later,"

"Come stand with me for a while,"

"They told me stories, my shoes did, talked to me all the time,"

"You don't look so fabulous, you look like you've got a leak too,"

"I'm sorry I was short with you last night, I'd just gotten rid of the shoes, and they were there when I did it,"

"The connoisseurs?"

"They kept me from jumping,"

"What do you mean?"

"After the shoes, they walked by just as I was about to do it,"

"I'm confused,"

"Maybe because they knew that they'd want me today, that their other guy had let them down,"

"Other guy?"

"They didn't say who it was,"

"Alfonso? The centaur?"

"They didn't say, just that they needed someone else, part time, for the odd job, I shouldn't have gone with them, I was enjoying my breakfast,"

"We have to go back there, Alfonso's a friend,"

"I don't know if it was this Alfonso,"

"He's a friend,"

"I'm not going back there,"

"It won't take a second,"

"Oh, I think it will take longer than a second,"

Solange smiled, winningly, and grabbed Ireneo by his generously muscled forearm.

NOT LONG AFTER IT HAPPENED, WHEN THE BLACK WOOL HE refused to take off even to sleep was still relatively fresh and the snow and ice covering the world was beginning to mix with mud and rain, Harry went for a walk that was remarkable only inasmuch as he was unable, even when he lost feeling in his extremities and every part of him began to ache and his lungs felt from one moment to the next as if they were being shot at with a nail puncher, either to reverse direction or stop until, thirteen hours after he had started, he staggered right, then left, then fell over into a large juniper bush, and although after his recovery he scoffed aloud when one of the counselors he had been assigned by his former company remarked that he had been "giving physical dimension to his grief," since that time he had envisioned his so-called grief as a long, terrible line frayed a little at the ends, an image that might help us to understand not so much how but *why* it was, as we move toward our own ending, that just as Solange and Ireneo, after very little discussion, turned around to go and see about the golden centaur, Harry emerged from a small street on the other side of the boulevard and, after a moment's pause brought on by his surprise at seeing them at all, let alone together, called out, but they had already turned and his voice was cut down by the poorly tuned chords of a sitar being struck with great vigor by a rather overdrawn bright-blue Hindu-swami sort of a statue, who had apparently rushed in to fill the void left by the Yellow Submarine, and in the seconds it took Harry to step through to the other side of the sound and the clearly skeptical fistful of people surrounding it, the two of them were disappearing around a thick, double-globed lamppost and striding off purposively, and although he had had it vaguely in mind to see if Alfonso (who was of course nowhere to be seen) would let him borrow back the submarine, or perhaps even give him one more ride in it for old time's sake, catching up with Solange and Ireneo immediately swept any other considerations aside, and in hopes of quickly closing the gap between them, he pressed his still nifty (though otherwise unremarkable) shoes into a fairly satisfactory lope, one that on a day when his mind was less encumbered by thoughts of racks hung with drippings, memories of glittering calderas, and small, wet arms and calves in the moonlight, might have made him think of his time as a secondary school football player, when anything he couldn't run past he could run through, unfortunately, immediately after successfully veering first past a chunky tourist sticking his fingers deep into a packet of candied oranges, then a bald man cradling the arm of a giant doll or mannequin no doubt shaken loose during the storm, then an ancient woman in dirty slippers slowly pushing a pram that held no less than five small, live, furred things, he was forced to stop by an enormous sparkling water truck that idled fully thirty seconds before pulling forward and clearing the way for Harry, who bolted forward so fast that he slipped on a pile of wet sand and twisted his knee and had to slow to a jog, which as it turned out was itself unsustainable, as, mere seconds after he had spotted

Solange and Ireneo again, now off at a troubling remove, he began to feel faint, then remembered he had eaten and drunk nothing since the odd meal the evening before, and of course his sleep had been wretched, and he had just spent an hour in the company of Señor Rubinski's drippings, and of course They were coming, and to make matters worse his voice was even less effective here in the face of a jackhammer that was smashing into the old stone ahead of him than it had been in proximity to the sitar, which is all to say that rather than closing the gap, as his initial burst had seemed to promise, said gap widened, with the result that the day's third instance of tailing was an almost perfect inverse of the first two, and even if the chance intervention of the memory of himself, standing in his brown velvet jacket at the bar thinking of stealing church bells and lying not altogether chastely beside a glamorous co-star, momentarily kept his mind out of the Rubinski's bathroom, Doña Eulalia's parlour, and the long-ago motel room in that world covered with snow, the reprieve was short lived, and if he hadn't chanced to look up just as the now-tiny figures he had almost forgotten he was following turned off the street into a building that seemed each time he looked at it as he drew nearer to have subtly changed not just its shape but its entire aspect, he might have taken one of the sharp turns his mind kept offering him and run into a wall or through a shop window or, as it had seemed to him the moment before he had fallen into the juniper bush, into a black lake ringed with snow, but in the event a few minutes later—having passed, without noticing him, Raimon in his Che Guevara costume emerging lost in thought from a side street—he stepped through the front door of the building into a courtyard lit even in the middle of the afternoon by globes of colored glass that rose along the undulating interior of the building, somehow deepening the smell of overripe citrus and damp stone wafting around him, not to mention the contrast between this enclosure and Doña Eulalia's, which had smelled like nothing more than cinders and had been lit only by a single bare bulb hanging from a cornice that now put him in mind of a description he had once read in which a man, lost in a blackness of the sewers beneath a great city sees a single chink of light in the ceiling far above, then strode forward to the stairwell where, his eyes having inscribed an arc that took them all the way up one wavy bank of windows then slowly back down the other, he saw what his peripheral vision had initially told him were three more of the globes: the pale faces of the connoisseurs pressed against the glass of a second-floor window grinning down at him.

B EFORE WE MOVE FORWARD, AS WE MUST—FOR THERE IS A
juniper bush waiting just ahead for us too—it is worth
mentioning that after Harry left the Rubinski's and stepped
out onto his filthy, sunlit street, no longer, at least not in
the short term, interested in sitting in his apartment and
waiting for another, even less commodious knock on the
door, or tap on his shoulder, the cold drippings of his darlings, he thought first of going to see Doña Eulalia again, of
attempting to ring a little more out of her, but while he had
no trouble at all this time in finding her building, the thick,
exterior door was locked tight and his pounding on it managed only to attract the attention of a group of women in
black housedresses and flowered aprons who had set chairs
against the side of the next building and were sunning their
heavy, mottled legs, and flicking at the air with black fans,
and while of course if it were helpful we could enter the
building and look in, as it were, on Doña Eulalia, it would
only be to find her in the grips of a sleep so deep all supposition was simultaneously made possible and irretrievable
in it, and while we might be justified in speculating that her
exertions from the previous night had forced her into this
slumber, we would do better to look closely at the unusual
glaze coating the well-sampled chocolate ducklings brought
the previous night by the manifestly persuasive connoisseurs, and hope that one of her relatives takes it upon
her/himself to look in on her, oh well, we have already seen

how her "Ah," was of some use, or seemed to be, to Ireneo, and it would have probably been asking too much to have expected her to come up with much more, though something like an "Ah" for Harry would have been quite welcome, just a little help—would that we who lurk in darkness could offer it to him, take him aside,

"Hello Harry,"

"Run, Harry,"

but it's possible the help he needs is already there, has already been offered and we have thus far missed it, at any rate, "They are coming," Harry thought and shuddered—with such force as it occurred that it tore a hole open in the blue door before him and he immediately ran through it and climbed the short flight of steps and stood behind Doña Eulalia's bed and put his face next to her lips and, although she was far away, she spoke, though it was only to repeat herself,

"They are coming,"

"I know, thanks a lot, thanks for nothing," Harry said—as he left Doña Eulalia's and decided, as we have seen, to make his way to the boulevard, and by chance his route took him past Almundo's Store for Living Statues, open for business despite the upended phone booth partially blocking its door and two gilt-edge panes from its front window that had been blown in and lay shattered in the midst of miniature cobalt skyscrapers surrounding an emerald Godzilla statue display, and before Harry quite knew what he was doing he had stepped in through the door and peeped around an immense pile of goblin masks and goblin finger puppets and saw, standing in the only clear space in the store—where he himself had been fitted for his own costume—the man with the fish-motif lapel pin who had spoken to him about golf on the plane, the man who had described the new ball that would allow him to prosecute such vigorous assaults, the man who had not been at all interested in Harry's comments about Restless Leg Syndrome and experimental invisibility, and who likely would have been even less interested in Harry's thoughts on the Black Dahlia, had he been able to articulate them, a subject, the Black Dahlia, which had slipped his mind since the apparition beside the Yellow Submarine of the young woman with hair mostly the color of crushed pomegranates, and did not seem at all auspicious in its resurfacing now, nor did the apparition of this, as Harry put it to himself, idiot, who, as he watched, suddenly let fall the golden golf club he had been holding frozen above his head, as if he were going to smash an invisible ball, and indeed when he more or less froze again, with the golden club now resting over his left shoulder, he had the satisfied air of someone who had sent an invisible ball roaring through an invisible landscape, and although the ball and its owner soon flew straight out of Harry's overcrowded head, for a moment it seemed to him that he could see it, this ball, that he was following it as it flew, faster and faster, past invisible parks and buildings and out over an invisible sea, where, rather than slowing, it picked up speed, so that he could no longer keep up with it, and was left to watch, if watch is the word, with considerable regret, as it went where he could not follow and where, before very long, it could no longer be perceived, which might have been the way that Solange and Ireneo would have put it had they been asked when, after stepping through the door of the building, the one that Harry would step through minutes after them, and making their way into the courtyard, where they couldn't help but stop to take in that space, simultaneously so awkward and elegant, with all its globes, which did not so much vanish a moment later when, recalling the urgency of their errand, they began to stride toward the stairwell—with Ireneo, who had found his courage, even if he would lose it again in a moment, leading the way—as reconfigure itself into the street they had just stepped off, though it took them a moment to determine this, as their orientation and position had shifted and they were now, rather than moving toward the stairwell, beside the jackhammer tearing up the street, and none the happier for the journey, in fact both of them nauseated by it, although Solange immediately turned back and, when she saw Harry now ahead of them entering the building, even began to run, and while Ireneo ran, as best he could in his espadrilles, alongside her, it was only to say that he was not interested in repeating the experience, that he did not think at that moment that he could, that his experience with the shoes had weakened him and he was sure that, if they returned to the courtyard, what had happened would happen again, that he thought that perhaps it was time he had a holiday, that perhaps he would leave the city and travel back up the coast to see his mother, whom he had not left in the best of health, even if she had not, in fact, been as sick as she had claimed to be, that he had had his running shoes on when he had stayed with her and had, as a result, perhaps not given her the benefit of the doubt when he should have, and a mother deserved that benefit,

"Undoubtedly," Solange said,

"Perhaps you would like to accompany me," Ireneo said,

"I'm going back there right now," Solange said,

"Well then, good-bye," Ireneo said, and he stopped and Solange continued, and, as she caught sight—though she couldn't quite believe it at first—of Raimon waving his cigar at her from down the block, she thought, "I will run so fast they won't see me coming," though unfortunately, in the event, they did.

THE STAIRS HARRY CLIMBED AFTER LEAVING THE GLOBE-LIT courtyard were made of fine marble and the banister with which he supported his sore knee was polished ebony and the walls were encrusted with gold leaf and mother of pearl and the door he decided corresponded with the connoisseurs, not least because it stood ajar, was a richly burnished slab of solid oak in the center of which had been sunk a peephole of cyclopean proportion, and if something like the smell of old fish hadn't seemed to emanate from it, Harry likely would have been more than mildly surprised to step out of all that careful elegance into a small, badly lit and even more badly ventilated room, on the filthy floor of which lay scattered more than one delicate fish carcass, along with miscellaneous small bones, scraps of paper, soda bottles, portions of moldy fruit, and a half-eaten box of brandy-filled chocolates, which one of the connoisseurs, who were still standing by the room's only window, picked up and held out to Harry, who looked at it for quite some time before shaking his head,

"Well then, fuck you, friend," the connoisseur said and lifted out one of the chocolates and handed it to the one of the other connoisseurs who popped it into his mouth and said as he chewed,

"What my colleague means is, welcome Knight of the Woeful Countenance, welcome to our fucking abode,"

"Thank you, I was following Solange and Ireneo," Harry said,

"Who aren't here," said one of the connoisseurs,

"Then perhaps they're in another apartment,"

"They're not in another apartment,"

"There are no other apartments, it's all offices, *this* isn't even an apartment,"

"This is our office,"

"Our orifice,"

"Nice, huh?"

"Connoisseur central,"

"Where we do our business, direct traffic, etc.,"

"Sorry about the mess,"

"It is messy," Harry said,

"Yeah, well, it's been a long week,"

"A long century,"

"I should go find Solange and Ireneo, I'm sorry to have troubled you,"

"They aren't here, not in this building, you won't find them,"

"Believe us,"

"Although if you want to step over to the window here in about five seconds, you'll see one of them,"

"Yeah?" Harry said,

"Come on over, stand between us,"

Harry went to the window and, with connoisseurs on either side of him, watched a rather red-faced Solange burst through the street door, hurl herself halfway across the courtyard, then vanish,

"What are you thinking she's good for?"

"Once more, twice?"

"Twice, at least, this guy's got real charm,"

"And she knows he's here,"

"She does indeed,"

"You sure you don't want a chocolate?"

"I should be going," Harry said,

"What's the rush?"

"Yeah, what's the hurry?"

"Alfonso's here too, in the other room,"

"Care to see him?"

"I bet he'd like to see you, he's not feeling too well,"

"Got something at the market, didn't sit right,"

"Alfonso's here?"

"That traitorous son of a bitch,"

Harry looked first at one connoisseur, then at the others, and then at his pale reflection in the window,

"What's he doing here?"

"Alfonso? we were talking,"

"Deliberating on the subject of loyalty, or the evils of being a blabbermouth,"

"Now he's resting,"

"I think I understand," Harry said,

"Understand what?"

"This, you three, I mean not exactly, but sort of, this is bad, right?"

"What's *exactly*? Who cares?"

"Not I, said the fat, fucking fly,"

"He's getting it,"

"You think so?"

"It's finally coming back to him,"

Harry looked at their reflections, took a deep breath then another then took a step backwards, and saw that the three of them formed a kind of tripod upon which, Harry thought, a terrible, almost invisible camera could sit and snap photographs of his misery,

"You didn't change the tires, right, wasn't that the story?"

"You had to take a little trip and you were a little busy and you didn't get the tires changed and, well, you know, wintertime, fuck,"

"I think I'd like to sit down, I think that would be very nice," Harry said,

"Well pull yourself up some fucking floor, make yourself at home, after all it was us you really wanted to see, wasn't it, and now here you fucking are,"

Here I fucking am, Harry thought then went and leaned against a vaguely slimy wall and crossed his arms over his chest, but instead of sinking he held his position and it was as if he had entered into one of those more or less desirable moments when the powers of hindsight offer themselves in advance and nothing is surprising, nothing is ever surprising again, not at all,

"Drippings," he said,

"Fuck yes," one of the connoisseurs said,

"Waiting for you,"

"Say the word and we'll get their drippings back on them, in fact, bammo, it's already done,"

"The word?" Harry said,

"The *words* is what he means, and technically you already said them, back there,"

"At the motel," Harry said,

"Cold night if I remember it correctly,"

"Which of course he does,"

"I remember everything, so do they,"

"You said 'Take me instead,' Do you remember saying that, Woeful Knight?"

"Yes," Harry said,

"Well, say it again and now we'll take you instead,"

"I meant to change the tires," Harry said, and as he said it he thought he heard an invisible shutter click above them,

"Who gives a fuck, that was twenty years ago,"

"I even had an appointment to get it done," Harry said,

"Of course you did, now say it again, and we'll get them for you and you can have a nice little visit and then we'll take you,"

"Why?" Harry said,

"You think walking up and down the boulevard is enough to float our boat, we want you, you're a classic case, you appeal to us, we said so in that postcard we sent you,"

"That postcard?"

"The one with the picture of the city on it,"

"That came years ago,"

"You took your time getting here,"

"We'd practically forgotten the whole thing, the whole sorry business,"

"I thought you said you remember everything," said Harry.

"Figure of speech,"

"Whatever,"

"Who cares?"

"The point is we had to walk by you in your Woeful Knight gear two or three times to get it, and then we thought, good, finally, let's do it now,"

"Why now?"

"What's wrong with now?"

"Is there something pleasant happening in your life that you wouldn't like to leave? Something agreeable? Something nifty? Something neato?"

Harry didn't answer and the connoisseurs, all of whom had been looking at Harry with satisfied grins on their faces, suddenly turned and looked back out the window,

"Here she comes again,"

"She's slowing down,"

"Looks like she's going to have a fucking heart attack,"

"Too much jam,"

"Not enough candy,"

"She should have accepted that gift,"

"Like the old lady did,"

"That old lady liked her chocolates,"

"Nice old lady,"

"Maybe that young guy of hers would have been spanking enough, for not accepting our largesse,"

"There's never enough spanking,"

"Amen to that,"

Harry, standing on his tiptoes, could just see the street door opening,

"Well, now that's interesting," said one of the connoisseurs,

"Yes, it fucking is,"

Harry took a step forward and saw that both Raimon and Ireneo were now with the indubitably persuasive Solange as she charged across the courtyard, and not for the first time since his interview with Señor Rubinski he remembered the old story of the monkey's paw and the story of the poor Black Dahlia and the word "DRIPPINGS" appeared in all caps in his mind, then he thought about Raimon and his hands and Doña Eulalia and her lemon crème cookies and the old women in black dresses and the bell that was still in his pocket and something came to him,

"He changed his mind, and now Raimon's running with them,"

"How the fuck do you like that?"

"I'm not sure I do,"

"Listen," Harry said, taking the bell out of his pocket, bending over, setting it on the floor beside him and giving it a whack, "I think I would like to see Alfonso, after all,"

The connoisseurs looked back at him,

"In a minute, back to business, say the words first," one of them said,

"Yeah, excuse us, you have our full attention, especially since you brought that fucking bell, now say the words first, that's how it works, we have to follow procedure,"

"They are coming," said Harry, and hit the bell again,

"Yes, they fucking are, but only if you say the words first, say the fucking words, and stop with the bell,"

"Those are the words," said Harry, hitting the bell once more,

"Listen, Knight of the Woeful Fucking Countenance, the fucking words are 'take me instead' and now for jerking us around with that bell you better add a fucking 'please,'"

Out of the corner of his eye, Harry could see smoke beginning to seep from their mouths and bits of blood drip from their lips and an icy lake opened up behind them and a car skidded off the road and slid sideways into it, and it occurred to him that perhaps what he was seeing now was one of the pictures the almost invisible camera had taken and that, in fact, he wasn't seeing anything, or not what he thought he was seeing, right this moment, at all,

"I'm going to go in and ask Alfonso if he'll let me borrow the submarine again and then I'm going to go and apologize to Solange for lying to her and I'm going to tell her about my kids, and then I'm going to buy those two guys a drink," Harry said, hitting the bell a final time, then walking toward the door,

"That's beautiful, fuck face,"

"Yeah, that's just gorgeous, now if you want to see those kids again, turn around, and say the words."

Harry didn't turn around and he didn't say the words though a moment later he wished he had because as his hand closed around the doorknob one of the connoisseurs emitted something like a snicker, which Harry understood quite clearly when he had the door open and could see what was in the room waiting for him on a filthy black couch they were sharing with a bloodied and unmoving Alfonso, which couch looked directly onto a large back-lit aquarium full of multi-colored houndfish and blood parrots that held his darlings' attention the way the television once had when they had used to sit in front of it in the early morning in the flickering half-light, all those years ago, in fact they seemed utterly mesmerized by the fish, which were doing nothing so terribly striking as they moved slowly in and out of synthetic coral and plastic sea-weed and a tower of bubbles that rose through the center of the aquarium like a column of air, and while it suddenly seemed imperative to Harry that he gobble them up with his eyes and take them into his arms, he was halted first by Alfonso's voice—which seemed, by some trick of acoustics, to come out of the aquarium and not from Alfonso's mouth—"You still owe me your story," and then by his own answer, given as he stared into the roiling water, "I think it's just getting started, here, right now," so that when, as he began to lower himself onto the couch and to lift his arms and open his hands and found himself back out on the street just a short distance behind Solange, Ireneo, and Raimon, the image that played on his retinas as he started to run was not of his darlings but of a brightly lit box in which dark things moved, and though, when having reentered the courtyard, he yelled, "I'm sorry, take me instead," he and these dark things were flung back out onto the street, where, as his friends came up and took his arms and breathed softly on either side of him, he stood for what felt like a very long while watching them.

COLOPHON

Ray of the Star was designed at Coffee House Press, in the historic Grain
Belt Brewery's Bottling House near downtown Minneapolis.
The text is set in Goudy Village

FUNDER ACKNOWLEDGMENTS

Coffee House Press is an independent nonprofit literary publisher. Our books
are made possible through the generous support of grants and gifts from
many foundations, corporate giving programs, state and federal support, and
through donations from individuals who believe in the transformational
power of literature. Coffee House receives major general operating support
from the McKnight Foundation, the Bush Foundation, from Target, and from
the Minnesota State Arts Board, through an appropriation by the Minnesota
State Legislature and from the National Endowment for the Arts. Coffee
House also receives support from: three anonymous donors; Abraham
Associates; the Elmer L. and Eleanor J. Andersen Foundation; Allan Appel;
Bill Berkson; the James L. and Nancy J. Bildner Foundation; the Patrick and
Aimee Butler Family Foundation; the Buuck Family Foundation; the law firm
of Fredrikson & Byron, PA.; Jennifer Haugh; Anselm Hollo and Jane
Dalrymple-Hollo; Jeffrey Hom; Stephen and Isabel Keating; Robert and
Margaret Kinney; the Kenneth Koch Literary Estate; Allan & Cinda
Kornblum; Seymour Kornblum and Gerry Lauter; the Lenfestey Family
Foundation; Ethan J. Litman; Mary McDermid; Rebecca Rand; Debby
Reynolds; the law firm of Schwegman, Lundberg, Woessner, PA.; Charles
Steffey and Suzannah Martin; John Sjoberg; Jeffrey Sugerman; Stu Wilson and
Mel Barker; the Archie D. & Bertha H. Walker Foundation; the Woessner
Freeman Family Foundation; and many other generous individual donors.

NATIONAL
ENDOWMENT
FOR THE ARTS

*This activity is made possible
in part by a grant from the
Minnesota State Arts Board,
through an appropriation by the
Minnesota State Legislature
and a grant from the National
Endowment for the Arts.*

MINNESOTA
STATE ARTS BOARD

TARGET.

To you and our many readers across the country,
we send our thanks for your continuing support.

Good books are brewing at www.coffeehousepress.org